PRAISE FOR KRISTINE GRAYSON

"With her series of magical romances, Kristine Grayson has carved out her own special and unique place in the romance genre."

— RT BOOK REVIEWS

"The reigning queen of paranormal romance."

— THE BEST REVIEWS

"...[Kristine Grayson] will have a long and glorious career."

— THE ROMANCE READER.COM

"Kristine Grayson gives 'happily ever after' her own unique twist!"

— KASEY MICHAELS

"Grayson's clever, humor-tinged writing is absolutely delightful."

— BOOKLIST

ALSO BY KRISTINE GRAYSON

Look for These Other Titles from Kristine Grayson

DRESSED IN HOLIDAY STYLE

THE SANTA SERIES

KRISTINE GRAYSON

DRESSED IN HOLIDAY STYLE

Once Upon A Time...
Not too long ago...but long enough to be somewhen else...

CHAPTER 1

RAINE WILKINS STOOD in the ankle-deep snow, staring over the hedge. The mansion's golden interior light spilled across the massive yard. All of the trees and shrubs beside the building were covered in silver fairy lights, with a touch of red and green, tastefully placed to hint at the season. A gigantic Christmas tree stood in the floor-to-ceiling bay window of the ballroom, but the other windows—also large—revealed couples waltzing as if they were extras in a Fred Astaire movie.

The women wore long dresses that flowed with their every movement, their hair short and styled or long and piled on top of their heads, held in place with tiaras and bows and jewelry that glittered. The men wore tuxes with tails that added to the sense of motion.

She could almost hear the music.

Someday, she would dance like that. Someday, she would be invited to these glitzy, glamorous parties. Someday, she would be one of the glittering women, swirling around the dance floor as if bred for it.

She wasn't bred for it, of course. She stood in the snow, her ancient boots starting to leak, her ratty (but warm) parka wrapped around her, her gloved hands tucked inside the sleeves, creating a makeshift muff. She had forgotten a hat, and she didn't want to put the hood up because it would block her vision. The parka was heavy-duty, the kind built for a good Midwestern winter, the kind they'd had when she was a kid, the kind the weather forecasters said they would have this year.

She shouldn't be here. She had told herself she would drive to the mansion in Lincoln Park just to see how long it took to get there from her ratty apartment on the Near West Side, knowing that tomorrow she would have to account for traffic as well.

But she had known, deep down, that she wanted to see the gala event of the season and imagine herself taking part, instead of standing on the sidelines, asking questions about the event—for, of all things, the Life and Style page (which her editor snidely called "the society page").

She hated Life and Style work. But, she reminded herself, unlike her colleagues from Northwestern, she had gotten a paying job as a reporter at the *Chicago Courier*, one of the few remaining big dailies in the nation, and she'd been promised that she could keep the job if she outperformed every other new hire from that summer.

Outperforming meant taking the humiliating work along with the good stories. Not that any good stories had come her way yet. She was too young and too new.

She was covering stupid stuff—high-end engagement parties, routine political speeches, and (her least favorite) the county fair. Often, she was doing background for one of the "real" reporters, or helping them post their articles on the paper's brand-new website.

She hadn't expected this. She had awards and credentials. She had written for major newspapers (with the prodding help of her professors), and she had interned at one of the most prestigious papers in the country—for no money, of course. She'd actually had to pay the university tuition for the privilege of interning, because the position provided "experience" and "enhanced her résumé" while infusing her with more cynicism than a woman of twenty-four should probably have.

She sighed. She wished, just once, she had some money and respect. She knew that the very rich people waltzing inside that mansion weren't the stuff of fairy tales, but she liked to imagine they were. The Rich—different from everyone else, if she were to believe F. Scott Fitzgerald. She liked to believe they not only had better clothes and more financial opportunities, but also perfect lives.

She'd never had a perfect life. She'd been so poor that she hadn't known where her next meal would come from. Not a lot of Northwestern freshman had homeless parents and full scholarships. She'd kept that secret, even from her best friends at school.

College had been a luxury for her, and her experiences growing up had enabled her to survive that disastrous internship without going either hungry or bankrupt.

She'd even freelanced. That had made her so much more money than her stupid job was earning her right now. Maybe she should give up the steady paycheck and strike out on her own....

"Aren't you cold?"

The male voice from behind her made her jump. Her heart rate increased a thousandfold, but she tried to pretend she wasn't alarmed as she turned to see who spoke.

A tall, blond man stood behind her. He was about her age, with flawless skin—the type she would have killed for—just starting to pink up from the chill, a square jaw, and blue eyes so electric they seemed lit from within.

Men this handsome didn't just lurk behind shrubbery.

Particularly men this handsome who were also wearing a tux as if they'd been born to it.

The white scarf wrapped around his neck appeared to be his only concession to the weather. He had his hands in the pockets of his tux trousers, but he didn't look cold.

She wondered if he was drunk.

"I feel like I should be offering you my parka," she said. "Isn't that the chivalrous thing to do?"

He shrugged one broad shoulder. "The chill feels good. It's stuffy inside."

"It'll feel good for a few minutes," she said. "And then you're going to regret you ever stepped out here."

"And regret that I joined you to spy on the Lifestyles of the Rich and Famous?" He didn't sound sarcastic, but in her mind, she could hear Robin Leach's smarmy voice blaring the words. She hadn't thought of that show since she was a kid. Even then, it had been a guilty pleasure.

Her cheeks heated. She'd been caught.

She decided not to lie. "It looks pretty in there."

"Oh," he said. "It is pretty, in a soulless, let's-make-this-the-most-stunning-room-in-the-world sort of way."

As if she knew what that was. She'd like to experience it, just once.

"You don't like it," she said, both as a question and a statement.

He shrugged again, his blue eyes looking past her. He was taller than she was. He could probably see inside so much better than she could.

"I've always liked that saying, 'Home is where the heart is,'" he said.

Something about the way he spoke the cliché caught her ear. She'd been concentrating so hard on not looking startled by him that she hadn't noticed, until now, that he had one of those indefinable European accents. An English-is-my-second-language-and-I-speak-it-better-than-you accent.

"You'd better go back inside before you freeze," she said.

He smiled faintly and looked at the windows. Their light reflected in his magnificent eyes.

"I'm not sure I'm going back in," he said.

She frowned. "Why not?"

He shrugged again. "I have a hunch," he said softly, "I'm about to run away."

CHAPTER 2

*R*AINE'S BREATH CAUGHT. People usually weren't that honest with her, especially when they had just met her. But she wasn't even sure he meant that comment for her.

He was still looking inside the mansion, as if measuring each movement.

"Run away?" Raine asked. "From what?"

"The pretension," he said, almost as if he wasn't talking to her. "The expectations."

Her inner reporter finally woke up. "What expectations?"

He blinked as if he were surprised that she was standing beside him. He smiled, faintly, dismissively, and the lost expression left his face.

He shrugged a third time.

"I take it they didn't let you in because of their rather stringent dress code?" he said.

"They didn't let me in because I wasn't invited," she said with a bit more bite than she expected. "Think of me as the Little Match Girl."

"I should hope not," he said. "She died at the end of that sadly misnamed Christmas story."

Raine's cheeks heated even more. She had forgotten the story's details. She'd only remembered the little match girl of the title, standing on a street corner, watching everyone else go about their business and ignoring her.

"Look," Raine said, "you have to get inside somewhere or you'll be the one who dies of hypothermia. And I don't have any matches to keep you warm."

He smiled. This time, the smile was real. It lit up his face. "I have a hereditary tolerance for the cold."

"And I have leaky boots," Raine said. "I also have a car, if you would like to go back to your hotel and get a coat or more comfortable clothes or something."

"I don't…." He stopped himself, then nodded. "A car it is. We'll stop somewhere to get you new boots and me something that makes me look like a twenty-first century creation instead of someone who stepped out of a Victorian Christmas party."

She smiled for the first time. He did look like the leading man in one of those black-and-white sketches from the pages of ancient newspapers. The actual society pages, back when there was some kind of society to look down its nose at everyone else.

Now, their descendants just danced in their finery and never thought of the sad impoverished souls standing outside.

Too cynical, girl, she thought to herself. *Don't say that stuff out loud.*

"I don't need new boots," she lied, "but I'll drive you wherever you need to go."

"'Need,'" he repeated. "Fascinating concept when applied to escape."

"I thought you said you were running away, not escaping."

He looked at her, then shrugged. He seemed to shrug a lot.

She wondered if he had developed his rather eloquent shrug language to avoid saying what he really thought.

"I think I need to experience Chicago during the holiday season the way the people really experience it, not...." He waved his hand toward that mansion, as if she understood exactly what he meant.

She didn't, not really. She wondered if the hand-waving gesture was like the shrug, something that allowed the listener to fill in the blanks so that the speaker was off the hook.

"And," he added, "if your boots are leaking, you do need new ones."

"Yeah, well," she said. "Need and afford are two different things."

He started, as if she had surprised him.

Her cheeks had grown so warm, she could probably qualify as her own heat source. He could put his hands on them and not need mittens. But she didn't say that.

She'd probably said too much already.

"Seriously," she said, "I'll drive you where you want to go, but you have to tell me where that is."

He nodded, then glanced over the shrubs. Then his gaze came back to hers. "I'd like to stop and buy presentable clothing. And I'd like to treat you to dinner."

She almost said that there were places in the city where tuxes were considered appropriate attire. But she didn't, because those places were so expensive she could pay half her bills with the cost of an entrée.

"You're determined to get out of here, aren't you?" she said. "I suppose your regular clothes are inside?"

It had taken her a few minutes to figure that out. Sometimes she was slow, but she eventually caught on.

He glanced at her, frowned just a little, and then smiled— that smooth, not-quite-there smile. "Um. Yes."

She got the sense that he hadn't quite lied to her, but he hadn't told her the truth, either.

"All right," she said. "Let's go to the car."

And, she thought, *get this very strange evening underway.*

CHAPTER 3

*S*HE HAD PARKED almost two blocks away because she'd been worried that there would be a guardhouse or security or something.

She suspected that if she had gone past the shrubbery, she would have discovered how intense the security really was. She had initially thought she would show up on some security camera somewhere, and they would watch her, maybe send someone out to get rid of her.

But now that she'd met this guy—whom she really hadn't met at all, just talked to—she was beginning to wonder if there was any security outside of the sculptured part of the lawn.

She trudged through the snow, past the other gigantic lawns and smaller mansions that lined this part of Lincoln Park. She'd parked just at the edge of this ridiculously expensive part of the city, where the less fabulously wealthy had condos or penthouse apartments instead of actual brick-and-stone buildings surrounded by perfectly coiffed snowdrifts.

The man walked beside her, head up, staring at the neighborhood as if he hadn't seen it before. She wondered at herself. Usually, she didn't pick up stray men and offer to take them somewhere in her car. Especially if she found them lurking in shrubbery.

Had she decided he was trustworthy because he wore a tuxedo or because he was the most handsome man she had ever met or because he just seemed honorable?

She had turned down dates with men she'd spent a lot of time with because she felt that she hadn't known them. And now she was doing this.

Then she shrugged—at least mentally—and continued forward. If nothing else, she might be able to get background for the story she had to write for the Life and Style section.

She rounded a corner, and there it was—her faithful steed, the car she'd managed to purchase from her old college room-mate, Verity. Raine had known it was a pity sale. Verity couldn't believe anyone could survive without a car, and had wanted to give Raine the car when her parents gave her the next year's model. But Raine couldn't stomach a free car, no matter how nice the gesture. So she had given Verity half of her savings—all $500 of it.

Verity, bless her, had signed a bill of sale, transferred the title, and said nothing. Then, anyway. She did later say (repeatedly) that Raine could borrow the money back at any time without interest or a payment schedule.

Some people, especially those who grew up in privilege, did not understand the importance of paying your own way.

But Verity's generosity did mean that the car Raine led this man to wasn't a total rust bucket. In fact, the car was only three years old and had more amenities than Raine's apartment.

She wrapped her hand around the key fob but didn't unlock the car. Even though she (weirdly) trusted this guy, she wasn't going to unlock the car without a bit of information.

"Before I drive you wherever," she said, "you have to do one thing."

The man looked at her, tilting his head as if silently

commanding her to continue. That communicating-without-talking thing that he did was both intriguing and irritating.

She wondered how that habit had developed.

"You have to tell me who you are," she said.

He stopped and jerked slightly, as if she had hit him with a mild Taser shot. He glanced back in the direction they had come, as if weighing her question.

"I'm Raine Wilkins," she said, and extended her mittened hand.

He relaxed visibly. He had apparently misunderstood her question. Had he thought she was asking for his résumé? His bank balance? His lineage?

He took her mitten in his bare hand. His skin hadn't yet turned red with the cold. She could feel the firmness of his grip through the wool.

"I'm Niko," he said, and that word had even more of an accent than anything else he had spoken. "N-N-North. Niko North."

The stammer was a surprise. And again, she had the sense of not-quite-a-lie coming from him. Or maybe she was losing that sense of trust, just a little.

They didn't really shake hands. They just held each other's fingers and looked in each other's eyes for a moment before she let go. Her heart started to flutter. She willed it to stop. That pitter-patter thing did not belong in this moment. She needed to keep her wits about her.

"And you're not from Chicago," she said.

"Is it that obvious?" he asked.

"I figured when you wanted to see how Chicago's other half lived, you weren't from the city. All the halves mingle here, whether we want to or not." She stepped over a pile of snow a plow had pushed against the curb and used the fob to unlock the car.

It chirruped at her, a friendly sound that she often

thought of as a *Hello! Welcome back.* She had never told anyone that either, not even Verity, who saw cars as possessions, not as sanctuaries (or possible places to live if things really got bad).

"I unlocked your side too," she said to Niko.

He nodded, pulling the door open and sliding inside. She got in as well.

The interior smelled of leather and coffee. She kept the car, in Verity's words, "disturbingly neat." Raine had detailed it after she bought it, and she kept it clean and ready for any emergency. Except for the day's coffee cup, which always sat in its little cup holder on the driver's side, the car had no garbage in it at all.

"What sort of vehicle is this?" Niko asked, running his hand along the dashboard.

How to answer that? It was a Lexus, which Verity had thought too "old" for a woman in her twenties, so the next car she got was some kind of sports car. Verity's father didn't want to give a leased car to a twenty-something, so he bought Verity's cars outright. Which meant Raine owned this thing, which had initially cost about $50,000 new. The *insurance* cost her more than the car had.

"Um," Raine said, "it's a sedan."

She hoped she hadn't insulted him. Guys usually wanted to know about car makes and models, but guys like that would ask a slightly different question, like, "What kind of Lexus is this?" rather than what kind of "vehicle" it was.

"Hmm," he said, touching the dash and then the leather seats. "It is astoundingly comfortable."

As if sedans couldn't be comfortable? Lexus's couldn't be comfortable? *Cars* couldn't be comfortable?

She let out a small breath, and turned the ignition. The car hummed to life. He watched her every move as if he hadn't seen anything like it before.

Maybe he watched everything like that, with a cool fascination that made it seem important.

And maybe she was overthinking this.

"You want clothes, right?"

He nodded.

She didn't ask where he wanted to go to shop. He had said he wanted to go downtown, so she took that to mean the Magnificent Mile. After all, he had been inside a Lincoln Park mansion and he was wearing an expensive tux.

The traffic was pretty light. It took less than fifteen minutes to get to the parking garage closest to Bloomingdale's. They didn't talk much along the way. He asked a few questions about Lake Michigan in the winter, and she answered them with the surety of a tour guide.

He kept his face turned toward the passenger window, watching the scenery go by as if he had never noticed it before.

She had chosen Bloomingdale's flagship store because she figured he could get everything he needed in a department store, and he wouldn't have to be outside long. In spite of herself, she was worried about him.

They got out of the car. She led him to the entrance. She said, "Just look at the signage for the men's department. I'll wait for you on the ground level in the coffee bar."

"You're not coming with me?" he asked, sounding vaguely lost.

Okay, she thought that was totally strange. She didn't want to see a man she didn't know well try on outfits. She wondered if he wanted her to pay for his clothing too.

She shrugged, hoping it was as elegant as his shrugs had been. "I got a bit of a chill. I need something warm. I'll wait for you there."

If he didn't have money, he would say so now. Or he would back out of this whole thing.

Or she could back out if he got weird.

She waited.

Instead, he smiled ruefully. "Ground level it is. I'll try not to take too long."

And he walked away from her into the bright store, all decorated for the holidays. He looked like a model, someone who had arrived at the store to pose for one of the high-end holiday ads—the kind that try to encourage rich people to give their friends and families cars wrapped in giant bows.

She watched until he disappeared behind a gigantic Christmas tree covered with white fairy lights and lots of Bloomingdales' ornaments. Then she took the escalator to the lowest level and walked into one of the more expensive coffee bars in all of Chicago. She was probably spending what she normally would have spent on lunch just for a cup, but she really did need the warmth.

The coffee bar smelled of freshly ground beans. Several shoppers sat at tables, leaning into each other and conversing softly over tasteful piano jazz versions of Christmas carols.

She ordered a cup of holiday mocha, pulled off her mittens, and stuck them into the pockets of her parka. Places like this always made her self conscious about her clothing. Her feet were cold and soaked inside her leaky boots, her parka had never been in style, and her mittens had been hand-knitted by her mom. At least she hadn't been wearing the matching hat, although her short bob was probably messed up from the wind.

Here, it wasn't fun watching rich people enjoy themselves, probably because they could see her spying on them and knew at a glance just how out of place she was. Here, she felt like her homeless teenage self, sneaking inside a place she didn't belong just for a bit of warmth.

She sipped at her drink, but mostly used the ceramic mug to warm her hands. As she warmed up, she slipped off the parka, revealing the bulky, hand-me-down sweater she usually wore on days she didn't plan to see anyone.

And of course, she was now shopping with the most handsome man she had ever met, a man who looked stunning in a tux, a man who had taken one look at her and decided to cast her in the best-friend role in a buddy comedy. She wasn't sure why that made her feel sad. She wasn't interested in him, was she? A man who was running away from a party, who hadn't really said much to her as she ferried him to his destination?

He hadn't even apologized for taking her time. The fact that she was annoyed about that one fact would have made her college friends from out of state laugh at her.

Overzealous apologizers, Verity had called Midwesterners. *If you don't start with an apology, you're considered rude.*

Raine's cheeks heated at the memory. Her blush response was getting a big workout today. She smiled to herself. Verity had been right: the default apology actually meant something to Raine.

The fact that Niko North hadn't done it was yet more confirmation that he was Not From Here.

"There you are."

She looked up from her steaming mug.

Niko was standing beside her. She hadn't seen him enter the coffee bar.

She had thought he looked good in a tux, but he looked even better now. He was wearing a pale blue, cable knit sweater that showed off his broad shoulders and flat stomach. He had tucked a pair of blue jeans into brown work boots. He had a heavy black coat draped over his shoulders. In his left hand, he held paper shopping bags with Bloomie's special holiday logo emblazoned on them. They probably held his tux and shoes.

With his right hand, he set down a beautifully wrapped package in front of her. The wrapping was white, decorated with a sparkly gold ribbon tied in a magnificent bow.

The box was huge. It looked like one of the fake presents under the Christmas trees decorating every floor of this mall.

She swallowed. Verity would still laugh. The Politeness Dilemma, she would call it. How do you say no to a kindness without insulting the kind person? Verity would've been blunt, but blunt wasn't coming to mind for Raine.

"I—um—what's that?" She suddenly hoped she had made an incorrect assumption. She hoped he wasn't giving her anything. She hoped he had bought a holiday gift for a friend or family member while he was here, and had simply set it on the small table in front of her.

The snobby rich people around her were watching surreptitiously from their tables. The conversations had trailed off, except for a pair of businessmen in the corner, discussing the day's latest stock reports.

"I wanted to get you something for your trouble," Niko said.

That blush that never entirely faded warmed her entire face. At least she wasn't cold anymore (except her feet. She wouldn't be able to warm up her feet until she got home).

She weighed her possible responses.

You didn't have to was Midwestern for *Thank you so much. You surprised me!*

I can't accept this was rude.

Thank you meant *I'm thrilled.*

So, she blurted, "It's been no trouble."

Even though it had been a little. She had gone out of her way to bring him here, and it had cost a parking fee and the stupid holiday drink, which she wasn't going to finish.

Niko smiled softly. The change of clothing made him look younger, more accessible, like an actual person instead of a male model. Plus, his blond hair was slightly mussed from pulling the sweater over his head, and it gave him a just-out-of-bed tousled look.

Her breath caught. So she *was* interested. Which was wrong in so many ways.

He glanced at the package, then back at her. He seemed amused instead of offended.

"My family specializes in gifts," he said. "We always give gifts, generally to people who never give us anything. It feels so good for me to give you something in return for your time. Please, let me do what my family does."

How could she say no to that? This was turning into the strangest few hours of her life.

She gave him a weak smile. "Okay," she said, and in that wobbly word, she could hear every doubt she'd ever had about him. He probably could too.

He set the bags down and pulled up the chair opposite her. He put his chin on his palm, tilted his head, and watched her fumble with the present.

It was bulky and a little heavy. She leaned back, and set her mug on the newly emptied table behind her, so she wouldn't spill liquid on the present.

"It's too pretty to unwrap," she said, hoping she would get a reprieve. She could open this at home, or figure out a way to stuff the present back into one of the bags. (Okay, that was rude, too. She would never do that, either. She was rather appalled that the thought had even crossed her mind.)

"Presents are always about the possibilities, aren't they?" he asked. "When they're wrapped, they can be anything."

Or nothing, she thought. She'd opened too many presents at the homeless shelters that had vouchers inside. She would rather have had the voucher directly, or in an envelope, than suffer through the anticipation of a present.

"But do open it," he said gently. "The wrapping is a lot less important than what's inside."

Her stomach clenched. Was he transforming into creepy stalker guy, doing inappropriate things just because she was nice to him?

The entire shop had gone quiet. She gave him her most brilliant smile (which felt totally fake) and then slid the present toward her.

She carefully untied the ribbon and draped it over one of the empty chairs. If she were honest with herself, that ribbon was too pretty to crumple up and waste on a five-minute package wrap.

She would take the ribbon and the wrapping to her parents' small apartment, the place they lived now that they had gotten back on their feet. Her parents still saved the tiniest things.

She willed thoughts of her family out of her mind as she slipped her finger under one of the pieces of tape and released the side of the wrapping. She loosened the rest of it to reveal a large, solid, cardboard box inside. She couldn't read the manufacturer's name—she had opened it from the wrong side.

The blood had left her face for the very first time in hours as she caught an inkling of what might be inside. She hoped that the clerk or the temp employee or whoever had wrapped this lovely present had just used a discarded box, maybe one from Niko's personal buying spree.

The box was for boots.

She unwrapped just a bit more, then slipped the box out of the wrapping, setting the paper on the seat of that empty chair. She peeled back the box's lid to reveal expensive waterproof boots that went up to mid-calf.

"I couldn't…" she started, then realized just how rude she was sounding. But she really couldn't. It was an outrageously expensive gift, especially from someone she had just met.

"I guessed at the size," Niko said, "but since we're here, we can just go up and exchange them if they don't fit."

"I can't…"

"You said your boots leak," he said. "That's just not acceptable."

It wasn't acceptable, but she couldn't afford boots—especially not boots like this. Despite herself, she ran her hands over them. She could feel the waterproofing, the thickness of the exterior, the warm fake fur inside.

She wanted these. She wanted them more than she could say. They were perfect—and they were in her size.

"We just met," she said so softly that, for a moment, she wondered if she had spoken aloud.

Niko let his hand drop away from his chin and sat up just a little. Then he added one of those eloquent shrugs. "I know. I acted on my culture's customs, not yours. I did not mean to alarm you."

His accent was a little stronger than it had been earlier. She wondered if that was deliberate.

"If I have upset you—"

"No," she lied. What was wrong with her? He had been generous. And no one had ever done anything like this for her before. Was it normal among the rich? Was it charity? Or was it something else? "You didn't upset me."

His gaze hadn't left hers. It felt like he could see inside of her, like he could see the lie.

There was no good way to say no to the boots. Except "no," Verity would have said. And honestly, Raine didn't want to refuse the boots. She'd had her leaky pair for two years. She often lined them with garbage bags, but she had forgotten to do that this morning.

She started, "It's just that no one has ever—" and before she could finish, he was on his feet, and walking toward the counter of the coffee bar.

She felt disoriented. The fact that he left was even stranger than the gift.

"—done anything like this for me before," she finished.

Although she wondered if that were true. Verity had essentially given her a car. But it had been a car that Verity—whose parents were filthy rich—would have either sold or traded in or abandoned in her second parking space.

Niko had bought Raine a gift—a thoughtful gift—on the basis of an hour's acquaintance.

She moved the boots to the seat of the empty chair and stared at them. She felt off-balance.

Niko returned, carrying a steaming mug.

"Sorry," he said, and for a very brief half second, she thought he was apologizing for the gift.

The overzealous apologizer in her felt satisfied with that, but another part of her felt disappointed. She didn't want him to apologize, not deep down. She realized she liked the gift, the special treatment.

Jeez, she was being weird. She simply did not know how to handle this at all.

She was fretting so hard she almost missed the rest of what he was saying. "I didn't mean to walk away, but that thing you were drinking looked so good that I just had to get one."

Before he sat down again, he grabbed her drink and put it back on the table. He glanced at the boots, and she wondered if he was going to comment on where she had set them. She hadn't even tried them on.

"I'm getting hungry," he said. "Is there somewhere around here where we can have a good dinner?"

Her expression must have changed for a very brief moment, because he frowned just a bit.

"Dinner had been part of the bargain for you bringing me down here," he said. "I offered to treat, if you'll recall."

"But with these boots…" she said.

His gaze slipped away from hers. "It was a spur-of-the-moment thing."

And she was making a bigger deal out of it than he was, apparently.

She felt stupid, but also odd. The boots had made her realize the risk she had taken driving him down here. He seemed nice—he seemed nicer than nice. He seemed *too* nice, if there were such a thing.

Maybe it was her problem (hell, it *was* her problem), but she'd read too many detective stories, watched too many true crime programs on television, and listened to stories from too many women she'd interviewed for the serious news stories she'd done before she got her "real" job.

Stalkers often started this way. They were too attentive right from the beginning. They found women like her, women who had had too many hard knocks, and then they treated that woman like gold. The problem was, they wouldn't leave her alone, even if she wanted to be left alone.

And instead of meeting Niko when she was at her work or even at her best, she had met him when she'd been peering at a party in a mansion, like a little kid who'd been forbidden to mingle with the grown-ups.

"I'm…afraid I'm going to pass on dinner." Raine just couldn't handle it. Yes, he was gorgeous. Yes, he was nice. And yes, he was odd. She was too cautious—too paranoid—to deal with odd.

(Or maybe she was too screwed up to deal with nice. She had to examine that as well—later, when he wasn't staring at her with those intense blue eyes.)

A tiny frown appeared just above his nose, adding to his attractiveness, weirdly enough. He didn't understand.

She didn't expect him to. She wasn't going to explain herself. They had just met, and things had gotten weird, and she—

Oh, heck, they'd started weird. *I'm about to run away.* What was that all about?

"I'll drive you anywhere you want," she said, "but I'm not comfortable with…"

She was going to finish with the word "you," which was half a lie, because she was comfortable with him—at least her body was. She leaned toward him, she thought he was attractive, she *liked* him.

But her brain and her survival instincts wouldn't let her go any farther. Too many red flags. And she didn't want to say that, because he'd bought her the boots. Because she found him attractive. Because she had the sense that he was *nice*.

"It's all right." He put his hand over hers. His fingers were warm and strong. "I understand."

Yet he said it in one of those tones that implied he didn't understand at all. Not that she blamed him. She wasn't sure she understood all of it either.

Just like she didn't understand why she wasn't pulling her hand away. She was sending mixed messages, and she felt vaguely guilty about that.

He took his hand off hers a half a second before she pulled away.

"And," he said, that accent still strong. "It's all right. You do not have to drive me. I will take a cab."

"You don't have to—"

"I do," he said. "I have made you uncomfortable. For that I am sorry. We do not really know each other, do we, and I presumed."

He inclined his head. The apology was there, and it was almost enough to get her to change her mind. She would have too, if there weren't butterflies gathering in her stomach.

"Thank you," she said, and stood. She wasn't certain if she was thanking him for being understanding, or thanking him for the boots, or thanking him as a reflexive gesture—the flip side of that Midwestern politeness: if in doubt (and *I'm sorry* isn't appropriate) say *Thank you*.

She stood, folded the wrapping paper and ribbon and placed them inside the boot box, and then slipped on her coat. She gathered the box against her chest.

"It was really nice to meet you," she said lamely.

His smile was sad. There were no eloquent shrugs to go with it. "It was nice to meet you as well."

She turned away before she could change her mind, and hurried out of the coffee bar. For a brief moment, she toyed with going back inside and trying to explain herself, but she didn't.

She rode the escalator up to the level where she had come in, wondering if she should return the boots and tell the clerks to refund his credit card. That would be the smart thing.

But she needed boots, and she had almost no money, and she decided that she could suck up her pride for this one thing, even though it felt odd.

Although she knew she would think of him every time she put on the boots, and she would wonder if she'd handled this entire situation correctly.

Maybe someday, she might even know the answer.

CHAPTER 4

*T*HE NEXT MORNING, she drove back to Lincoln Park. The press conference was being held in the reception room of the large mansion she had spied on the night before.

The mansion was open to the public in the holiday season, just so that the unwashed could see what kind of decorations someone with money could slather all over a ten thousand square foot home. Raine had gone once, years ago, with her college friends, who'd oooed and ahhhed over each little bauble.

She hadn't oooed or ahhhed. She had walked through in thin-lipped silence, noting how much clothing (or food) each doodad could have bought for children like the one she had once been.

She had a hunch she would be even less happy to be here this morning. In addition to the expensive doodad Christmas show, the press conference was bogus make-work, just like most press conferences she attended for the Life and Style section. This press conference was being held by an international conglomerate with the cutesy name of Claus & Company. Some corporate bigwig was making an announcement about Claus & Company's new gift-giving program for people in need.

She had been to so many of these things that she had tuned out before she had even arrived. She had to pay attention, at least a little, because the only way she could write a story different from every other low-level reporter's was to find an angle all her own.

And it couldn't be the new angle presented at the conference, because TV reporters would be here too. Mansions like this one, all decorated for the holidays, and press conferences from corporations like Claus & Company made for great evening news visuals. The reporters who had a brain would often pull the one new thing from the half-hour-long conference, and blare it on every half hour iteration of their newscast.

If she wrote the same thing as the evening news blare, the morning paper would look like a repeat of whatever it was that the local stations had covered the night before.

And her editor would be very, very unhappy.

He had already rejected the first angle she had proposed: How the holiday gifts for needy children never went far enough—how those kids needed the basics year-round, not just at the holidays.

Hey, Scrooge McDuck, he said to her. *That's also an evergreen story. We all know impoverished kids lack everything. We run that story sometime in the middle of December. But events like this one are happy-feely stories that put the smile in the holiday season.*

She didn't feel like smiling. She felt grumpy. She hoped an angle would suggest itself once the stupid press conference was over.

She parked on the grounds of the mansion this time—there was no real security now, and there wasn't a glut of cars. Even though the sun was out, creating slush where there had been snow and ice the night before, her feet were dry because she wore the boots Niko had bought her.

They fit perfectly, almost as if they had been made for her. She had never had boots (or even shoes) that fit so well. The interiors were warm and soft, and her feet felt good inside them.

And true to the realization she'd had as she left the coffee bar, she thought of Niko as she pulled the boots out of the box.

She half-hoped he had run away like he said he would. She didn't want to see him. She was vaguely embarrassed by her behavior the night before, even though, if she were presented with the same circumstance right at this very moment, she would respond in the exact same way.

That didn't block the guilt she was feeling at keeping the boots—and at treating him like he had done something sneaky, when he was probably just being kind.

It was the "probably" that concerned her.

So it would be best if he weren't here. If he was, she would simply ignore him.

Although she hadn't ignored him even in her own mind. She thought of him long before she put the boots on. She thought of him when she dressed in her pale pink work sweater (sparkly and trim), black pants that would tuck into the boots and accent her legs, and her very best coat, the one that made her look like she had stepped out of some 1940s holiday movie.

She walked up the stairs to the double oak doors, which stood open. She double-checked, like she always did before walking into a press conference, to make sure she had her microcassette recorder as well as the notebook she always used to scrawl bits of information.

Because this conference had been designed with TV people

in mind, a well-dressed flunky greeted her at the door and took her coat, handing her a ticket and telling her the coat check was gratis. Raine had done this enough to know it was also required, so that everyone, even the print reporters, looked good on camera.

She watched her coat disappear into the bowels of a huge closet and then she walked past two large Scotch pines. Their fresh scent made her think of Christmas. Despite her holiday history, she always found that scent to be full of hope.

White and gold-gilded signs on brass floor stands pointed the way to the press conference. She had to thread past several portraits of people she did not know, evergreen boughs looping over everything, and an antique grandfather clock that was probably worth more than the building she lived in.

By the time she reached the large hall where someone had set up a stage with a podium, she was already sick of the holiday excess. She wanted to turn around and leave, but knew she didn't dare. Two doors, behind the podium, were closed. A worker had just finished putting up a backdrop with the tasteful Santa logo of Claus & Company (which suggested but didn't copy the Coca-Cola Santa of fifty years ago). About fifty chairs stood near the stage, some with reporters already seated in them.

She passed a table laden with a dozen different kind of Christmas cookies, some candied fruit, sliced quick breads, and finger sandwiches. Behind the food, beautiful silver urns sparkled, labeled *coffee, decaf, tea,* and *water*. This spread didn't have the usual bottled waters and soft drinks visible on the table. She suspected that they weren't being provided because they weren't attractive and because they were a little bit déclassé.

Then she shook her head at her own thoughts. She was snobby in the reverse. The mansion itself put her on edge. Maybe that was why she had been so cold to Niko the night before; she had been deeply uncomfortable. There were two parts to her: the part that envied every single person who had danced in the mansion the night before, and the part that thought those people were heartless souls who did nothing of value to help others in need.

Oh, she was in quite a mood going into this press conference.

Before she found a chair, she walked up to the podium and put her voice-activated recorder on it. When she was in college, she'd always had to search for her recorder at the end of a press conference. The reporters from the "big" newspapers would continually move her recorder farther and farther away.

Now, her recorder was labeled with the *Courier's* name, and no one dared touch it. She always arrived a little early so that no one would know that the *Courier* had sent a fresh-faced cub, who looked more inexperienced than everyone else in the room.

She chose a chair in the back, partly because she was grumpy, and partly because she knew better than to fight with the TV people for the plum seats.

Some flunky had placed a folder on every chair. The folder contained a press release inside, along with some still photos of Claus & Company's headquarters, Christmas trees with piles of gifts beneath the lowest branches, and some headshots of corporate staffers that she didn't bother to look at.

Other reporters were filing in. The TV people were already setting up, adding their mikes to the taped pile of mikes on the podium, and finding a place to stand that wouldn't block the camera angles of their competitors.

Raine pulled out her notebook and pretended to be writing about the ambience as the rest of the reporters found their seats. Around her, everyone complained softly about the lack of bottled water and the worthless nature of the press conference.

Precisely at 11:00 a.m., a nervous little woman wearing a red-and-green suit bounded up the two steps leading to the temporary stage. She stepped behind the podium, but only the top of her head was visible over it. So she stepped to one side, making every reporter on the opposite side of the podium groan a little. They couldn't see her anymore.

The camera operators, standing in the back, shifted as a unit, but without a lot of energy. Everyone knew that the people who introduced usually didn't provide the important information in the press conference (if there was important information, which Raine doubted there would be).

The woman had bright green eyes, and a pointed chin that made her face seem quite narrow. She tucked a strand of blonde hair behind her ear, then turned to see someone just outside of Raine's line of vision. Raine stared at the ear. How did they find someone with tastefully pointed ears to introduce the press conference's Important Personage?

Obviously, no one at Claus & Company was leaving this press conference to chance.

"Welcome, ladies and gentlemen," said the woman in a voice as tiny as she was.

Or perhaps the folks at Claus & Company liked visuals better than anything, since the little woman's voice was getting softer as she spoke. She looked like an elf, and while that would play well on television, it didn't help everyone else in the room.

"Use the mike!" one of the radio reporters yelled.

The woman beside Raine muttered, "Don't bother," as if she were talking to the radio guy, even though he was two rows up.

That little kerfuffle made Raine miss most of what the tiny woman said. Her voice got lost in the shuffling and the muttering. Her face had turned as red as Raine's had the night before. The little woman looked terrified.

She glanced to the side again, and then said something inaudible, and extended her hand to one side.

The TV reporters in the front row sat at attention. Apparently, the little woman had finished her introduction. She looked at the reporters as if surprised that they hadn't applauded.

Raine actually felt sorry for her, and wanted to tell her that reporters only applauded for the president of the United States, and then, only out of politeness (and fear) when they were inside the White House briefing room.

A man walked out of one of the doors in the back. He wore a chambray shirt and dark blue jeans, along with tennis shoes. Raine expected him to adjust the microphone or move the podium. Instead, he stood behind it.

Her breath caught. It was Niko.

He looked older and more polished. The comfortable jeans and shirt gave him an authority that the tuxedo hadn't.

Some of the TV people frowned, craning their necks to look for the person who had just been introduced. In Chicago, no one who spoke at a high-level press conference ever dressed in jeans. Suits, ties, maybe shirtsleeves in the deepest, hottest summer, but never looking like he had just set down a wrench in the back room to come out and make a point.

Niko smiled softly as he watched them. He knew what they were looking for, and he knew they didn't see it in him.

"Thank you for coming," he said, without leaning into the mike. His rich voice was perfectly suited for speaking to a crowd.

Raine felt a shiver run through her. She wanted to bend her head over the notepad she had brought, but she also didn't want to look away from him. She wasn't sure why he looked better every single time she saw him, but he did. Which meant she had to be really careful when she dealt with him.

"Every year," he was saying, "Claus & Company sponsors charity events in major cities around the world. For the past decade or more, these events have been managed through our charitable arm. In that, this year is no different. What is different—as should seem evident to all of you who are still looking for the Niko North that Falda introduced—is me."

The heads of the reporters who had still been looking past him snapped into place. A few of the cameras moved sharply toward him as well.

His smile remained, but his eyes twinkled.

Raine frowned. That twinkle almost seemed like something fake, as if it had been produced by a flare of light behind him or an effect someone had designed on the podium.

No one's eyes twinkled like that, not in a way that would be visible several rows back.

He paused for a moment. "Now that you realize I'm the person you've come to see, let me explain who I am."

Raine was gripping the pen as hard as she could. When she realized the pen was bending, she set it down, stretched out her hand, and then picked the pen back up again, all without looking directly at it.

"I am, as Falda said, Niko North. My family has owned Claus & Company for more years than I care to think about, certainly as long as the company has done business inside the United States."

She let out a small breath. He owned Claus & Company? No wonder he thought the boots were a small token. Their cost represented pocket change to him.

"My father, who is in charge of the company, is beginning to make noises about stepping down. He wants a family member to take his place. Throughout the history of the company, that family member has been the oldest son. My mother has finally convinced my father that's no way to run a business in this modern era. She believes the business should be run by a family member, but the family member best suited to the business, not the family member who was born first."

Everyone was staring at him now. A few of the TV reporters had signaled their camera operators to move slightly closer. A couple of print reporters were scrawling as fast as they could.

Raine glanced at what she had written which was only one word. *Owns?*

She let out a breath. Already this was less of a fluffy press conference than she had expected. She hoped the microcassette recorder was getting most of this, because she had been too busy staring. And processing. And wondering why the hell he had wanted to run away the night before.

"I have five siblings. All older." Niko tucked his thumbs in the back pockets of his jeans.

Raine realized suddenly that the casualness was a pose, as much of a costume as the one he had worn the night before. He was pretending to be comfortable. His posture said he was being open.

But his posture lied. He was deeply uncomfortable. He was just hiding it well.

"Two brothers, three sisters," he was saying. "And all of us have received an assignment this holiday season."

Then he inclined his head to the right, as if someone had contradicted him. His smile became self-deprecating.

"Well, to be accurate," he said, "we have had assignments during the holiday season throughout our lives. This year, the assignments are large and designed to reveal our strengths and weaknesses."

The room was silent. Everyone seemed riveted. Raine knew she was.

"Clearly, one of my weaknesses is the ability to prevaricate. I don't, if I can avoid it. Which is why I am telling you all of this now. It is, believe it or not, an introduction into the remarks the marketing department at Claus & Company has prepared for me. The remarks that I'm sure someone in the back is shaking at me right now, as if I were the most dense person on the planet."

Then he turned slightly, and grinned to someone off-stage. Everyone else looked too.

Raine couldn't see anyone, but she didn't know if that was because of where she sat or because that person remained just inside one of the doors behind the stage.

Niko turned his attention back to the reporters, removed his hands from his pockets, and gripped the podium. The radio journalist one row ahead of Raine winced. That sound would have boomed into every single mike in the place.

"With our corporate mandate comes freedom," Niko said. "We can run our little fiefdom anyway we want."

Fiefdom. That was an interesting word. Raine wrote it down.

"I am in charge of Claus & Company's charitable efforts in the City of Chicago this holiday season. Each of my siblings will handle holiday charities in five other large cities, each in a different country, and each with different holiday traditions. We are allowed to run the charitable efforts any way we see fit. For example, we can continue to follow past procedures."

His smile softened as he made eye contact with the reporters in the front row. Someone had trained him to speak in front of a crowd, and how to use it for good effect.

"I'm sure," Niko said, "my father would prefer that approach. One of his favorite sayings is one you're all familiar with: If it ain't broke, don't fix it. Of course, being my father, he would say: If it's not broken, leave it alone. He is a stickler for rules, even grammatical ones."

For a moment, Raine saw the man she had seen the night before, the one who felt constricted by the circumstances. Raised among people who followed rules, Niko probably wanted to escape, if only for one evening.

Maybe he had been afraid of what lay ahead. Even though he was trying to put a good face on all of this, he seemed uncomfortable with what he was facing. Or perhaps he was just thinking aloud about the challenge.

She wished she could see the marketing department representative in the back. She had a hunch that person had his face in his hands right about now, silently cursing Niko for causing problems within the "fiefdom."

Even using that word probably would cause a lot of problems. She smiled, and then leaned back, not wanting him to see her.

"However," Niko said, "I think Claus & Company is stuck in the past. We've been a very successful company for a long time, but a lot of our success came in the middle of the twentieth century, and, quite frankly, we're coasting."

She started scrawling. She had to keep this. There were too many sound bites for the TV people. She would be able to write her own piece—maybe an "uneasy lay the crown" kinda thing.

She felt an itch behind her shoulder blades, which she often got when she was considering something she shouldn't. Niko hadn't known she was a reporter last night. But they had had an experience together. She was wearing the proof. And she could mention how uncomfortable he had been with the corporate shindig that he was supposed to attend—the one he had run away from.

She could write about that moment. She could mention that he was seen leaving the party, and heading into downtown Chicago. Because he was seen, and not just by her. She was certain clerks at Bloomingdales would remember him as well, especially when he had come in wearing that tux.

Her cheeks heated. What she was considering was journalistically ethical, but personally suspect. He had been kind to her.

But, of course, she had been kind to him as well. She had

driven him away from the party in an untraceable way. She had helped him run away, if only for an evening.

"Speaking for me, and me only," Niko was saying, "our charitable works are the most important part of our business. The charity work doesn't bring in revenue like the licensing and the endorsements. It's not as flashy as the movies and the pop-up books. But charity is at the heart of our business. We started with charitable acts, back in the dark ages of our business, and we have continued those acts. I want to change them from a pro forma way that our company behaves to something proactive."

Raine frowned, and looked up. Her movement must have caught his attention, because their gazes met.

His smile fell away for a moment, and his skin lost its healthy color. He went pale.

She could tell what he was thinking: He had spent the evening with a reporter. She actually saw the edges of fear in his expression.

Then his smile returned and his gaze left hers, seeking out some other reporters'.

"I'm sure all this is too detailed for the average press conference," Niko said. "I am clearly not the best marketing representative from our company—especially judging by the reaction of the staff in the back."

He turned toward them again, grinning this time. His hands left the podium and his thumbs returned to his back pockets. A nervous gesture, a tell.

"So, I guess I'll return to the script." Then he chuckled. "If actually speaking on script for the first time could be called *returning* to the script."

Raine's mouth had gone dry. That itch in her back was worse than it had been a few minutes ago. He knew, as well as she did, that she could reveal his evening of doubt.

His father sounded like a true stickler for details. That little escape might forever destroy Niko's chances to head the company.

And Raine held the power in her hands to change the course of Claus & Company. Niko had given that to her, as clearly as he had given her the boots.

"Normally," Niko was saying, "we hold charitable events like the one last night. We charge money so that patrons of the arts or large donors can have an evening of entertainment in return for their gifts."

Something in his tone caught her attention again. Was that sarcasm? Did he think as little of those events as she did?

Surely, she had asked the people in charge at her first chari- table giving press conference years ago now, *donors could just pony up funds for the poor without being rewarded for it. Isn't giving its own reward?*

Ah, the flunky in charge of that press conference had replied, *we have an idealist in the back. I do wish the world worked that way, my dear. Unfortunately, it does not.*

"We also have large toy drives, sponsored through several of your organizations. Thank you for that support, by the way." Niko sounded more relaxed as he said all of this, but he was clearly working on a script now. "We work with the food pantry to provide holiday meals, and with a variety of charities to make sure that everyone has warm winter clothing."

Raine tensed. Had she been a charitable case to him? Someone to provide for? Had she misread the entire interaction?

That wasn't like her, but then again, she hadn't had a lot of experience with people who were natural philanthropists, either. She was used to the hard-bitten reporters or the over- whelmed workers in soup kitchens.

"I don't have trouble with the organizations we work with," Niko was saying, and then he glanced over his shoulder. Someone was probably going crazy. That sentence was clearly off script once again. He stepped slightly forward, as if trying to get the marketing person out of his range of vision.

Raine kept her pen poised over the page. She had a hunch this was going to be the money quote. And yes, it would probably appear in the evening newscasts, but she didn't care. She could take room and expand on this.

"My problem," he said, "is not with what we do. We're extremely effective at it. We have a great success rate. Fully ninety-five percent of our funding goes directly to those in need."

Impressive. Even the best charities often spent as much as 25 percent on overhead and expenses. The lights had to stay on, and the people who ran the charities had to feed their families as well. Some charities—particularly those that were science-based—also had to factor in research costs.

"Clearly," Niko said, "we're well run. We have great support worldwide. So, I suppose you're wondering what my issue is, why I'm rambling on about changes."

Raine's pen was still poised over the page. She *was* wondering, and she would wager everyone else in the room was as well. But no one was asking, which was pretty amazing, considering the room was full of reporters.

Niko had them mesmerized.

"My issue is with our mission," he said.

Someone moaned loudly behind him. Apparently, the person in charge of keeping him on message had finally lost it.

Niko grabbed the podium again. The radio reporters winced a second time.

"Our mission is to make certain everyone has a wonderful holiday season, no matter what their economic status is, no matter what their religion is, and no matter where they live. Obviously, we miss as much as we succeed, but in the last thirty years, we have greatly improved the health and happiness of millions over the holidays."

Now, Raine was frowning. Much as she complained about holiday-only charities, holiday help was often all the help families in need got, particularly the working poor. She waited for the other shoe—boot—to drop.

"I believe we need to maintain that mission and add to it," Niko said. "We shouldn't start the charitable giving anew each November. We should be helping those in need year-round."

Some of the print reporters started to shift in their seats. She could see hands preparing to shoot up.

"Now, granted," Niko said, "many of our partner organizations already help year-round. But they don't have as much success fundraising for other times of the year as they do during the winter holidays."

He leaned into the mike. The expression on his face was intense.

"I want to put Claus & Company's muscle behind the fundraising in Chicago year-round. I also want to raise money to set up housing for the poor and co-op grocery shopping in areas without large supermarkets. I have a plan that will begin this year, and will continue throughout the next five years. We need to take our vast resources and—"

"Do you really think it's wise, Mr. North, to funnel money away from the existing charities?" asked Richard Rancone, one of the TV reporters who specialized in confrontational shows.

"I never said we would funnel money away," Niko said. "I hadn't gotten to the funding yet—"

"Because a lot of people rely on those charities," said Gerda van Halstad, another one of the confrontational reporters. "If you take money out of their mouths—"

"I'm *not*," Niko said. "I'm proposing an increase in funding. We're going to—"

"It sounds like you're breaking a system that already works," said another TV reporter, clearly not wanting to be left behind. "You're—"

"I have materials," Niko said. "I'll have one of my assistants pass them out now. I—"

Reporters stood, shouting questions, and Niko's face turned red. Raine was used the feeding frenzy. She also knew that the misunderstandings often led to better TV and better ratings than accurately covering the news conference.

She also knew that Niko had given the reporters enough to destroy him. If they judiciously cut the speech he'd been giving, it would sound like he was actively taking food out of the mouths of children.

She shot to her feet before she even realized what she was doing.

"Mr. North," she said in her loudest voice. It cut through the noise. "How much will your new project cost?"

He looked at her with such disappointment that she almost sat down. She wasn't sure what the cause of the disappointment was. The fact that she had asked that question? The fact that she was a reporter? The fact that it seemed like she had become part of the feeding frenzy? Or all of the above?

"It will cost an extra one hundred million dollars to start," he said.

"An *extra* one hundred million dollars," she said, just so the confrontational TV reporters got the point. "Who is providing the start-up money?"

His features relaxed visibly. He realized she was helping him.

"Claus & Company," he said. "We have a general charitable giving fund. I received permission to start my vision with a donation from that fund—"

And there he was, getting lost in the details again, details that never made for good sound bites.

"So, Mr. North, you're telling me that you will not be using *any* of the money collected for holiday charities to fund the start-up charity, is that correct?"

He swallowed hard. "Yes, Ms. Wilkins."

She wished he hadn't said her name. Now she looked like a shill.

"Can you guarantee that, Mr. North?" she asked. "And before you answer, realize that my paper, the *Chicago Courier,* has a one-hundred-year history of going after fraudulent charitable claims. Our investigative journalism department is the best in the city."

That last wasn't for him. It was for everyone else. *I might look like a know-nothing reporter*, she was telling her colleagues, *but I work for the biggest newspaper in Chicago, and they don't hire slackers.*

"I can guarantee that," Niko said quietly. "My work on this plan predates my family's new edict. I have hated the holiday-only nature of our charities for years. Children don't get enough food year-round. They don't have a place to put their heads in summer as well as in winter. In fact, more children starve in the summer than they do in the winter, because they lose the opportunity to have one good meal per day—lunch at school."

"I see you've done your homework, Mr. North," Raine said. "But homework is different than a plan."

He gave her a sideways smile, one she recognized as genuine. "It is indeed, Ms. Wilkins. As you can probably tell, I am not the best spokesman for all of this, and when I went off script, I probably blew any opportunity to sell this to the people of Chicago correctly. So let me be really clear."

He paused. The other reporters remained quiet, waiting. Raine prayed he would speak in a single sound bite, because if he got too complicated, he would blow his final chance with these people.

"Claus & Company is proud to continue the charitable work we have done every holiday season with our local partners. In addition, we are adding a new year-round charitable arm, which we shall fund-raise for separately. We have chosen the great city of Chicago to begin our year-round pilot program because we believe we can do a tremendous amount of good here."

Someone had clearly written that. Niko had finally used the script. He had barely stayed within the thirty-second sound bite, but he had managed it.

"If I give one hundred dollars to your charities," the radio reporter one row up shouted, "how much of that will go this new program?"

Niko stared at Raine for just a moment, as if she could help him answer, then he looked at the radio reporter. "You will be able to designate which charity your hundred dollars goes to. Claus & Company's Holiday Fund will exist as it always has. To support Claus & Company's Uplift Fund, you would need to specify that your money goes there."

Uplift Fund. He hadn't even mentioned the name until now. No wonder the marketing people in the back were going nuts.

"I get to choose?" Gerda van Halstad asked. She sounded confused.

"What if I want fifty dollars to go to one fund and fifty dollars to go to another?" asked another reporter almost at the same time.

"Isn't that needlessly complicated?" asked Richard Rancone.

"I'll answer you first," Niko said to Rancone. "We need to keep the charitable arms separate because their missions are separate."

"And you don't believe in the Holiday Fund's mission, do you?" asked Rancone.

"I do believe in it," Niko said with great exasperation. "Didn't you hear what I said? I just want to add to it. I want us to help people year-round. What's so hard to understand about that? It's part of Claus & Company's mission, and we need to do it right. It's a pilot program, something that will benefit Chicago."

"You sound defensive, Mr. North," said Rancone. "What aren't you telling us?"

Niko looked at Raine again, as if she were behind the questions. Or maybe because he needed a friendly face.

She shrugged slightly. Niko's lips tightened in obvious frustration.

"What am I supposed to say to that?" Niko said to the reporter. "You're trying to create a crisis where there is none. I'm here to help—"

"So you think Chicago can't handle its own problems?" Van Halstad asked.

A chubby man in a coal-black suit came out of the back. He headed toward the podium.

"I didn't say that," Niko said, moving his hands in a what-in-the-world gesture. "I said that we're starting a new charitable arm—"

The man in the coal-black suit actively pushed Niko aside.

"Thank you, Mr. North," said the man in the suit. He had the same odd accent Niko had. "I'm Jørgen. I handle North American marketing for Claus & Company. Let me explain what we're doing here. We let Mr. North handle this press conference because he will be running the charities—"

"Better than he ran the press conference, I hope," said Rancone with a grin.

Niko put up a finger, as if he wanted Jørgen the marketing director to shut up. Niko leaned toward the mike, but Jørgen blocked him again.

The pretty elf-like woman came up to Niko's side and tugged on his sleeve. He shook his head. Then she grabbed his arm hard, and pulled him away from the podium.

The TV reporters were gesturing toward their camera operators, making sure that they got this.

Jørgen was trying hard to pretend nothing was happening around him. He smiled sadly, and said, "We wanted you to know that the North family is one hundred percent behind this. As you can tell, Mr. North is not a practiced speaker. He is the most honest man we know. He's perfect to run the Uplift Fund, because he will deal directly with everyone, just as he has here."

A group of well-dressed young people appeared. Raine had no idea where they had come from. Maybe they had been waiting in the back. They moved to the edges of the aisles, handing out folders.

Jørgen was speaking loudly. "We are passing out materials on the Uplift Fund. We're pleased to start this new charitable organization. It's going to make a large difference here in Chicago, and, after a trial run here, throughout the world."

Raine took one of the folders and passed the others to the reporter next to her. The folder was green, with a red label marked *Uplift Fund*. She sighed. Someone should have handed this out with the first folder.

Whoops.

Raine let out another small sigh. This press conference was a disaster. Normally, she would have chuckled, and then turned it into a big joke when she got back to the news room, but she didn't feel like it this time.

Niko had been unprepared—or unwilling—to do what most PR flaks did, and it had hurt him. It might have hurt his dreams.

She felt bad about that.

She also wasn't sure what she would do next, either. She had the ability to make the situation worse, score a big coup for her paper, and launch her career out of the Life and Style section.

But Niko's dream, the ability to put a lot of money behind a year-round charity that might do something for the city, was also important to her.

She slid the new folder behind the other folder. She would spend a little time in the afternoon investigating the plans, and then she would consult with some of the people she knew who advised charitable start-ups and see if they would comment on the record.

That was something she could do that the TV people couldn't. She could do an in-depth piece. She would hand the in-depth piece to her editor at the same time as the straight coverage of the disaster press conference.

She took more notes and waited for the marketing director to get done so she could retrieve her microcassette recorder.

She realized, as she waited, she already knew what she was going to write.

And it wasn't going to include yesterday's adventure.

As handsome as he was, as smooth as he seemed, Niko North lacked social skills. That had been apparent yesterday when he had given her the boots, and it had become even more apparent at the press conference.

She found that a bit more endearing than she wanted to.

She didn't want to think that she owed him, even as her feet were snug in those boots. And she also didn't want to derail something that might help thousands of people in her city.

She hadn't expected the ethical dilemma. She hadn't expected it to twist her stomach up as much as it had.

And she hadn't expected it to make her reporter self examine whether or not her childhood circumstances were getting in the way of her objectivity.

She could hand off the story to someone else. That would take care of the ethical issues—kinda.

Because she would have to explain to her editor why she was taking herself off the story, and putting herself in the position of researcher instead of writer. And if she did that, then the story of Niko North's attempted escape from his obligations would hit the press and have an impact she couldn't control.

Withholding that information, though, might get her fired.

She clutched the files.

She had some thinking to do.

CHAPTER 5

*W*HEN THE PRESS conference officially ended, Raine grabbed her microcassette recorder, and started to leave with the other reporters. The TV reporters had cleared out long ago to prepare their stories, while someone from their organization remained behind to retrieve the mike and the other equipment. Some of the print reporters were gone too—the older ones who never used recorders but took copious notes, mostly in some kind of personal, indecipherable squiggles.

She made it to the door before she stopped. She had an idea.

She doubled back to find two of the young people who'd been handing out folders picking up the debris on the floor. She was about to ask them to find Niko North for her when Jørgen the marketing director came out of the back, talking with the pretty elf-like woman about contacting Claus & Company.

"Excuse me," Raine said. "I'd like to speak to Niko North."

Jørgen gave her a withering glance. "I'm sure you know, miss, that we're not going to let any of you speak to him today."

She expected that. "I'm not just anyone. I'm Raine Wilkins

with the *Chicago Courier*. I spent yesterday evening with Mr. North."

"You and five hundred other people, Miss Wilkins," Jørgen said.

The pretty elf-like woman tugged on his sleeve, just like she had with Niko.

"Not now, Falda," Jørgen said.

"Oh," Raine said with a smile, "you might want to listen to her. What she wants to tell you is that Mr. North left the event early. No one could find him for hours. I drove him downtown, where he bought a nice sweater and some jeans so he could look like a regular person."

Jørgen's eyes widened. The pretty elf-like woman was biting her lower lip.

"And," Raine said, lifting her right leg, "he bought me these lovely boots."

Jørgen looked alarmed. It took him a good ten seconds to regain control of his face.

"We don't believe in tit-for-tat press coverage," Jørgen said. "You don't owe us anything. I'm sure you noticed that Niko doesn't understand the rules—"

"What I noticed," she said, "was how unhappy he was. He was talking about running away…."

Jørgen rolled his eyes. "Oh, *great*. Just great."

Falda, the pretty elf-like woman, tugged his sleeve again and nodded toward Raine.

Jørgen glanced down at her and said, "Well, he won't have that concern shortly."

"What?" Raine asked.

Jørgen looked at her, as if surprised she was still standing there. Then he shook his head. "What do you want to discuss with him, Miss, that I can't help you with?"

She hated the "Miss." The first couple times she was willing to assume he had misspoken or mispronounced "Ms." with that unusual accent of his. But now that he kept repeating it, she knew that he meant it. She felt more than a tad belittled.

Besides, she wasn't sure how she could answer the question he asked. Part of the reason she wanted to see Niko was to discuss the ethical dilemma he had put her in. She wanted to apologize in advance for anything she did that might hurt him.

Her cheeks heated as she realized that was one of her underlying motives. She was about to say something when the Jørgen rolled his eyes again.

"Wonderful," he said. "This just keeps getting better and better."

He had clearly misunderstood her blush to mean that she had had some kind of intimate relationship with Niko.

She let the misunderstanding hang.

"Go get him, Falda," Jørgen said to the pretty elf-like woman. "And tell him—oh, jingle bells, I don't know—just tell him to get his rear out here."

Jingle Bells? Rear? This company tried to present itself as squeaky clean, and that had even gotten into the language.

"You, young lady," Jørgen said to Raine. "You have to understand I will be standing here as you speak to him, keeping track of every word. I will interrupted, and I will keep this interview on track—"

"No, you won't, Jørgen." Niko had come out of the back. His hair was mussed and he looked rumpled. "I'll talk to her alone."

"No," Jørgen said. "Our rears are already in a sling because of this fiasco. I'm not going to have you make it worse."

Niko sighed. "Raine," he said quietly. "You didn't tell me you were a reporter."

"You didn't tell me you were a mogul," she said.

Niko gave her a half-smile, then nodded. He stepped down from the podium. He stopped a foot away from Raine. His clean scent seemed stronger than it had the night before. "You can leave us, Jørgen."

Jørgen shook his head repeatedly, like a misbehaving child. "I can't—"

"Look, it's not going to matter." Niko sounded tired. "I promise I won't say anything untoward."

"You'll forgive me if I don't believe you," Jørgen said. "You wouldn't know 'untoward' if it bit you—"

"*Jørgen,*" Niko said. "Please. Give me a moment."

Jørgen jabbed a finger at Raine.

"Young lady," he said (and she wanted to smack him, she really did), "you will understand that everything Niko North says to you, and I mean *everything,* is off the record."

"That's not necessary," Niko said. "Besides, there are some things I want to clarify."

"That's what I was afraid of," Jørgen said. "You will not clarify. You will not add. Is that clear?"

"No," Niko said. "It's already—"

"How about this," Raine said to Jørgen. "I'll consider this interview off the record if I can use some of the information as deep background. If I believe that some of the information needs to be attributed to Niko, I will have you look at the quote. Provided you work within my deadlines."

She stared at the Jørgen.

He stared back.

Niko was frowning. She wasn't sure he understood anything she had just said to Jørgen. But Jørgen clearly understood her.

"I didn't think the *Chicago Courier* let its subjects review quotes before they were printed," Jørgen said.

"We don't normally, but this isn't a normal situation. Besides, I'm not planning to do anything controversial here," Raine said. "I just want to talk to Niko. If that's what it takes to have a conversation, then I'm willing to compromise."

Jørgen shook his head. Then he brushed his hands together, as if he were clearing dirt off them.

"This is your mess, Niko," Jørgen said. "I'm making some notes so that I don't get fired."

"Family doesn't get fired, Jørgen," Niko said.

"But they do get demoted," Jørgen said, "and sometimes that's worse."

Raine frowned. They were related? They looked nothing like each other.

"If you screw this up even worse than you have," Jørgen continued, "then you answer to your father, not me. And I wouldn't want to be anywhere near headquarters when that conversation happens. He's already upset—"

"He knows about the press conference?"

"What part of 'he sees you when…' do you not understand, Niko? Sweet candy canes, man, you grew up with this."

Sweet candy canes? Really? Did people *say* things like that? Raine frowned. And quoting old Christmas standards? Was that for her benefit? Did Claus & Company always maintain a fiction that the company was headed by the real Santa Claus?

Niko was shaking his head, looking even more frazzled than he had a moment ago.

"Well," he said after a moment, "If he already knows, then I can't make this worse, can I?"

"Normally, I would agree, Niko," Jørgen said, "but this isn't normal, and it's you we're talking about, not your siblings. You have a talent—"

"For making things worse, I know." Niko ran a hand through his hair. "Is all of this off the record, or does the charming Ms. Wilkins get to use our fight in her newspaper as well as my quotes?"

Raine held up a hand, deflecting the worst of this. "I just want to talk to you."

"Go for broke, Miss Wilkins," Jørgen said. "Clearly I can't protect young Niko from himself. But then again, I was warned. They said no one could, and they were right. Come on, Falda. We have some damage control to do."

Raine watched them walk toward the back, the chubby man in the handsome suit and the tiny, pretty elf-like woman. The man put his hand on her shoulder, and she reached over and touched his fingers with her own.

"A press conference is just a press conference," Raine said to Niko. She felt bad for him. She shouldn't, but she did. She wanted to calm him a little. "This one *was* out of control and it'll dominate today's headlines unless some politician decides to leave his wife for his mistress or something dumb like that. But, even if nothing supplants this story, it won't last beyond the twenty-four-hour news cycle. Something equally juicy will happen tomorrow, and next week, and the week after that. So it's really not important."

"Not important." Niko let out a bitter laugh. "You don't understand. My family is all about press coverage and image. Some would say that's all we are."

She frowned at him. "Would you say that?"

He shrugged. Elegant, noncommittal, just like the night before. A don't-ask-me shrug.

"We do amazing things," Niko said, "but most of those never reach the media and probably should never reach the media. Claus & Company became an international business over a hundred years ago, and did it through clever marketing. I mean, we'd always had an international arm, but not an international money-making arm."

He waved a hand as if dismissing his own words. She frowned, realizing she knew almost nothing about this company—and she thought she had researched it well the day before.

"It doesn't matter. I get lost in the details and that's probably the biggest problem of all." Niko paused then peered at her as if focusing on her completely. "I'm sorry. You said you wanted to talk to me?"

He looked sad. She hadn't expected it, the way the planes of his face flattened, the slight downturn to his mouth. His features looked odd in this position. Normally, they looked like they were made for smiles.

When she didn't speak up right away, he said, "I didn't mean to bribe you with the boots. That's what Jørgen thinks I did. He thinks I'm just a screw-up. I really meant those as a gift. That's what my family does best. We give gifts."

He had told her that before. Her frown deepened, partly because she still felt an urge to soothe his feelings. She shouldn't feel like that, particularly in the middle of an interview, even an off-the-record interview.

She gave in to the feeling and raised one foot. "They're comfortable," she said, looking down at the boot. "And I'm grateful."

"They don't leak?" he asked.

"They don't leak," she said.

He smiled, just a little. "Well, I did one thing right, then."

She almost corrected him. It hadn't been right; it hadn't felt right; and now, because of the boots, her integrity was being called into question. And so was his.

Which brought up the reason she wanted to talk with him. She sighed softly.

"Look, Niko," she said. "I had no idea who you were last night—"

"I know," he said.

"And you clearly had no idea who I was," she said.

He nodded.

"But we know now," she said.

He froze in place, as if expecting another blow.

She continued, "Technically, because I was a part of the

events last night and an eyewitness to everything, I can write about them. That's perfectly legal in my profession."

His expression hadn't changed, but it had solidified as if he were afraid to move his facial muscles as well as the rest of his body.

"I'm…uncomfortable doing that," she said. "Maybe because neither of us identified ourselves correctly, maybe because of the boots, or maybe because it felt like a moment out of time."

His eyes followed her. Otherwise, he seemed like a statue.

"I…um…I like the idea of the Uplift Fund, and despite what I said about the press conference, this rollout might hurt it. I really don't want to do more damage, but I'm obligated—"

"To pile on, right? Like those other reporters?" His face moved now. His cheeks were red, and his blue eyes snapping. He was furious.

She held up a hand to calm him. He stopped talking, at least.

"No," she said. "I don't specialize in gotcha journalism. Which is why I'm uncomfortable about last night. Something was going on with you, and I'm not going to ask you about it, not that you could answer on the record anyway—"

"I just knew it," he said, as if he couldn't stop himself. "I just knew it. I just knew I'd screw this all up, and everything would go wrong, and I wouldn't pay for it, all those kids would. I just knew it, and they're talking about sending me home, and that's exactly what's going to happen."

His hand formed a fist and pounded the air as he turned away from her.

She was startled by the outburst. "Claus & Company is shutting down the fund?"

He pressed the fist against his face.

"Oh, not really," he said around the fist. "What they're saying already is that they're going to see how the donations go. But they're not going to push it, and the pilot program will fail before it ever gets off the ground, and it's because of my ego. I thought I could handle the press conference. I wanted to do something different, so the press conference wouldn't be standard, so it would get the media's attention, and damn—I mean, dang—I mean, zowie—I did that, didn't I? I got the media's attention."

She was stuck on the correction. *Damn, dang, zowie?* What was with this company, this family?

"Yeah," she said softly. "You did. And not the way you wanted."

"You think I don't know that?" he snapped. "Je—Fu—Fudge."

He sighed and shook his head, his hand still in a fist.

She was frowning, going over what he had just said.

"I'm sorry," she said, relying on the Midwestern apology as a transition. "You said they're going to pull the plug?"

"Not officially," he said, head down. "I mean, we just announced the roll-out."

"But the support is gone now?" She was trying to understand that. It didn't make sense to her. "That seems awfully fast, doesn't it? Shouldn't they give a new project more than a press conference?"

His smile was bitter. "'Awfully fast.' Oh, Ms. Wilkins, you don't know my family, and the things they can accomplish faster than anyone else in the world."

Her frown deepened. "What do you mean?"

He shook his head. "My family never bides its time on anything. We do what we need to do when we need to do it, or so my father says. And while they understand that building takes time, they also understand that execution has to happen quickly."

She wasn't sure if he was making a pun. "Execution?"

"Making whatever they're building happen. The goal, the end game." He snorted. "No one wanted me on this project. No one wanted this project, period. I was going to prove myself, and I did. I proved just what a screw-up I am."

"Surely, that's not the case," she said, not sounding like a journalist at all.

"Oh, let me introduce myself again, Ms. Wilkins." He extended his hand. She took it, and felt a sizzle of electricity. "I'm Niko North, the baby of the North family. Coddled and beloved until someone decided I needed to grow up, and then it became clear that all that coddling had made me incompetent. I need to start on the bottom rung, no matter what my mother argued—or at least the bottom rung for my family, which means the toy factory, which means assembly, which means more screw-ups because I can't use my hands like that at all. I'm all brain, dense and screwed-up brain, but brain nonetheless, so I'll be stuck in the factory forever if I go home, subject to the wrath of my father, and then, when he retires, the mercy of my siblings, whoever takes over the company, and my future is set. Oh, joy."

He hadn't let go of her hand, and she wasn't letting go of his. They felt connected by more than just skin.

"Based on one press conference?" she asked.

"And a lifetime of negative expectations." He sighed, then looked down at their joined hands. "You know, you're the first woman I've met in the Greater World outside of planned events?"

"The Greater World?" she asked.

"Oh, now I've slipped and given you the mindset of my family. There's our world and your world, which is called the Greater World. Ours is tiny but important, a little fiefdom in the middle of a vast fairy tale, that everyone seems to believe in but me."

He had used the word *fiefdom* in the press conference.

"What do you mean?" she asked.

He let her hand go. She felt the separation like a personal

loss. It took two seconds too long to pull her hand back and let it fall to her side.

"I'm not supposed to tell you. I'm not supposed to say half the things I've just said, none of which probably makes sense outside of the context of my family or the company, but oh, well. It's off the record anyway."

He took a deep breath and smiled. The smile was sad, but real, not like some of his earlier smiles.

"What I was going to say," he said, "before I tripped again, and mentioned the Greater World, was that I enjoyed spending time with you yesterday, even if you found it weird, and I only acted the way I did because I liked you, and did you know that when you're cold, the tip of your nose turns red? I think that's charming. I think you're charming, and I didn't mean to put you in an awkward position. I know you want to talk to me about that position, and about reporting what happened, and about how strange it all was, and how I was running away, and all I want to say is, go ahead. You can't hurt me, Ms. Wilkins. I've managed to do that all by myself."

He nodded at her, then turned and walked away, just like he had done in the coffee bar.

"Wait, Niko," she said. "I want to—"

He waved a hand behind him, then turned around, still walking away, *backing* away, actually. "We probably won't see each other again. They're going to send me home. That's what they do with screw-ups. So let me say this, thanks for trying, and for caring enough to talk at least, and thanks for those few hours yesterday when I didn't have to think about—"

He waved his hand at the room, as if indicating it. But she knew what he meant. He meant the press conference, his family, and the big to-do.

"Thank you, Raine Wilkins," he said. "It's been my pleasure to know you."

And then he turned and left the room.

She was alone among the chairs and the Christmas trees and the leftover equipment, some folders scattered on the floor. She couldn't see him anymore.

His pleasure? He had meant that. And they had had a strange encounter the night before. It wasn't one of the best times she'd ever had, but it was one of the most memorable.

And he, he had been interesting, and strange, and attractive.

She closed the hand that had touched his, still feeling the warmth of his skin on hers. She wanted to go after him, apologize, take him for coffee or lunch or get him out of here.

Everything she wanted had nothing to do with her job, or his job, or anything they could do.

He had walked away.

She needed to as well.

Once Upon A Time...
A little closer to now...

CHAPTER 6

THE WORLD CHANGED, like it always does.

Raine wrote the press conference story, did the analysis of the Uplift Fund, not that it mattered, because, just like Niko predicted, the Fund never really got off the ground.

For years, she wore the boots from the day the first snow fell until the day the snow melted, and as she predicted she would, she thought of Niko when she put the boots on, and sometimes, when she walked through deep drifts or cold slush, she thought of him too, because her feet remained warm and dry.

The boots lasted longer than her job at the *Chicago Courier*, longer than the *Courier* itself. The *Chicago Courier* tried to make the transition to digital, but failed mightily, and blamed the Internet—although Raine wondered if the problem was the fact that Chicago had two bigger dailies, and a third simply couldn't handle the competition.

Not that it mattered to her; she had left the *Courier* before it had left Chicago, hired away by the first of several hard-news start-ups that never quite made it off the ground.

As a hobby, she started blogging under a pen name about

non-hard-news things, almost magical things, combining her hard-news research habits and her love for the strange. Initially, she had planned to call the blog the Daily Raine, but decided against it when one of her start-up bosses found out she was going to write the blog and tried to claim ownership of it.

Instead, she used an alias and set up her website as a separate business, difficult to trace. She called the site *Fiefdoms and Fairy Tales*. She asked for donations to support it and didn't hire staff, although she occasionally wrote under more than one name to give the appearance of a larger company.

By the time she started the blog, she no longer lived in Chicago. She had moved to Washington, D.C. for one of her start-ups, then to New York for another, and finally to Los Angeles for a third. She kept her apartment in LA when she started the blog, but she realized that the cost of living in California was double that of her hometown.

Besides, she didn't count fire and flood as seasons. She preferred rain and heat and snow. She didn't like LA. She wanted to go back to Chicago.

It had taken a while for her to decide to move, however, because she had been so very poor when she had lived in Chicago. Her memories of Chicago were tied to her memories of poverty.

She had to clear those links—and clear the thoughts of that girl who had stood in the snow in leaky boots, watching rich people dance.

She didn't have enough money to buy a mansion, even though she made more money now than she could have imagined back in her leaky-boots days. In fact, she made a lot of money, more than her editors had made at the *Chicago Courier*, more than some of the local TV people made, as well.

But her income was based on donations and freelance articles, and she didn't trust it, knowing it could all change in a heartbeat. She had a lot of money socked away, enough to make a sizeable down payment and still have money (earning next to nothing) in savings.

She knew she was being too conservative, but that was the result of her upbringing. It still had an impact on her every single day.

It didn't stop her from taking some risks, though. Like leaving the L.A. Basin and moving back to the Midwest. Like freelancing. Like setting out on her own, something her parents had never done.

She finally settled on one side of a duplex near Lincoln Park, not too far from DePaul University. The neighborhood alone made her feel rich. The duplex added to the feeling, since she was in a brownstone with some history and a lot of extra room. The three bedrooms, narrow living room, and newly renovated kitchen made her feel like she had hit some kind of jackpot.

She had finished moving during October, as the leaves were turning colors and falling with each rainstorm. She had forgotten how much she loved the smell of decaying leaves, how nice the cool crisp air was, how nice the scent of wood smoke from fireplaces truly was.

She spent her days walking even when it rained, familiarizing herself with the changes in the city. Once, she had known it as well as she had known her own body. Now, she was relearning where some things were, what had been moved, and what had disappeared.

When she unpacked, she found her boots. She somehow had managed to keep them through all the moves and through the purging of possessions she went through as she went from tiny Los Angeles apartment to tiny Los Angeles apartment.

She set the boots near her door for the day of the first snow, which arrived a day earlier than predicted.

And, as she pulled on the boots, she thought of Niko North,

just like she always did. And she wondered, just like she always did, what had become of him.

She had begun her blog way back when, as a means to track down information on Claus & Company. She had learned that it was a closely held private corporation that did not release much financial material to the media. From what she could tell, it made billions in annual revenue on a variety of projects, had more charitable arms than she could track, and had offices in every major city in the world.

The company also had a huge media arm, which she ran afoul of whenever she made even a passing negative mention. Other blogs would appear, refuting her claims or explaining them. Not that she minded. Whenever Claus & Company's media friends mentioned her, her blog traffic increased. When her blog traffic increased, so did her donations.

She found it odd that she would profit from negative publicity. She knew that some of her fellow bloggers would often plant negative stories inside their blogs for that very reason, and she fought hard to remain as objective as she could, even when someone was throwing money at her.

She also kept what proof she could for her claims. She had no corporate backers, no legal team at the ready, and so she felt the only defense she had against defamation or libel charges was the research and links that she had found.

She carried that philosophy through all of her posts. She had done an exposé of a business called the Archetype Place in Anaheim, which seemed to have all kinds of strange characters working for it. As far as she could tell, the people connected to the Archetype Place believed they were archetypes, or at least had magic, like the people from the original fairy tales they resembled.

Through the Archetype Place, she discovered a man who many were convinced was the actual Prince Charming. He owned a bookstore. Of course, she couldn't prove he was

Prince Charming, any more than she could prove that his ex-wife was Cinderella. Raine had to dismiss the strange things his daughters told her as fancies of young, lonely little girls.

But Raine had glommed onto the phrase "The Greater World," which they had all said, just like Niko North had.

She couldn't track down the usage of "The Greater World," but it bothered her all the same.

She thought of that phrase, too, when she put on the boots the day of the first snow, just before Halloween. The boots were as warm and comfortable as she remembered, even though she could have sworn her feet had grown in size over the years. (The shoe salespeople told her that was normal—everyone's feet spread with age. She was beginning to hate those "with age" comments, particularly since she was clearly no longer a young, cute reporter, but a woman with crepe neck and crow's feet, who didn't quite look her age, but didn't look like she was twenty, either.)

Raine slung on a heavy winter coat, grabbed her gloves, and stuck a knit cap in her pocket. She hated wearing anything on her head. She had ear muffs if she needed them, but she hated those, too. She liked the coolness against her scalp. She would only put on her cap when the tips of her ears felt like they were about to freeze off.

She knew she had probably overdressed for her walk, but she didn't want the blast of cold that would hit her as she went outside to derail her daily exercise.

She loved the walks. Every day, they took her somewhere new. On this day, she had chosen to walk the few miles from her home to Old Town. Even though she had driven to some Second City and Steppenwolf Theater performances in the area, she hadn't walked the neighborhood. It had looked, from her brief dashes from a secure parking space to the theater, like the neighborhood had gentrified since she last lived in Chicago.

It took a while for her to get to Old Town proper. She meandered her way there, taking North Avenue and North Wells only when she couldn't avoid them any longer.

She walked past restaurants she hadn't seen before, smiled when she saw the tobacco shop was still in its place. She had done a Life and Style profile on the owner, and had learned that back in the day, it had been a head shop, selling drug paraphernalia, but as the owner had outgrown his marijuana habit, so had his customers.

Raine couldn't go inside, because the smell of tobacco made her sick, but she loved looking through the window at the beautiful humidors and the sculptures. She was glad the shop remained, since so much of the neighborhood had changed.

She headed down the tree-lined street, looking at some of the other businesses, ones she did not recognize. As she went farther, it became clear that the Old Town rents had gone up near North Wells, but not in the outlying parts of the neighborhood. Sketchy shops with only a bit of shelf space looked like they hadn't been in business long, and that made her smile, pleasing her almost as much as the first thick, wet flakes of snow.

The flakes fell faster than the usual Christmas snow because they were so heavy. As the flakes fell on her, they melted, and she knew she couldn't be out here long because she would get soaked. Still, she turned her face toward the pillowy gray sky, and let the snow chill her bare skin.

She had stopped walking. She turned in circles like a child in her first snowfall, feeling that same joy. Only she wasn't jumping or extending her arms or crying out with happiness. She was trying to maintain some semblance of adulthood, not that it mattered. It had been a long time since she had known anyone here.

"Nice boots," a man's voice said.

She started, and looked around for the source. She didn't

see anyone. Some cars drove by, sending slush flying, but no one else was on the rapidly darkening street.

She was about to walk away, when the voice added, "Do they leak?"

The accent was faintly European, as if the speaker had learned English on the Continent. A tingle ran through her.

She probably should have assumed that the speaker had just stumbled on words tied to the boots' history and walked on, but she couldn't leave, not without looking.

Besides, that accent caught her. How could that voice have all three elements she associated with Niko North? The warmth, the clipped European words, the knowledge of her boots?

She swallowed, and searched for the voice. It had come from in front of her. She saw a shadow in a doorway not too far from where she stood. The shadow moved, and her heart pounded. It was clear the shadow belonged to a tall man, whose features she couldn't quite see in the twilight.

She took a few steps forward, and the man stepped out of the doorway.

Her breath caught.

It was Niko.

His blond hair was longer, brushing against his collar. His face was thinner, and his skin had gained some sun damage, so he didn't look quite as perfect as he had years ago.

His smile seemed more sincere, though.

"Raine?" he asked.

"Niko?" she said.

And the next thing she knew, they were embracing like old friends who hadn't seen each other in years. That electric feeling caught her again—she had forgotten it—and she backed up, quicker than was probably polite.

He had taken a step back, too, and ended up beside the plate glass window with the words *Uplift Foundation* etched on it.

She pointed to them, feeling surprised. "So your family let you run the charity after all."

"Oh, no," he said. "I haven't been in contact with my family in years."

She felt a pang of sadness. She was alone too—her parents having moved too far away for casual visits—and she felt it as the holidays approached. In the past, she had tried to hook up with a new boyfriend long about Halloween, but then she realized she was acting out of need rather than desire and resigned herself to a life alone.

"I'm sorry to hear that," she said.

Niko shrugged. She had forgotten the shrugs, and how communicative they were. That had been a let's-change-the-subject shrug.

"The snow's coming down pretty hard," he said. "There's a great coffee shop nearby."

"Shades of the past," she said.

He smiled.

"Don't you have to stay with your—what is it? A store? An organization?"

"It's five," he said. "I've shut down for the day. I was just heading to my car when I saw you."

Then he raised a finger and touched it to the side of his nose. She flashed on a painting she'd seen in a child's book illustrating the poem *A Visit From St. Nicholas,* "laying his finger aside of his nose…"

She glanced around to see if there was a chimney nearby, but there wasn't.

Fanciful. That was her problem. That had always been her problem.

"You know," Niko was saying, "I still owe you dinner."

She smiled. "These are the same boots that you bought me," she said. "I've worn them for years, and they've been wonderful. So if anyone owes someone dinner, I owe you."

"Well, then," he said, "let's go somewhere lovely and haggle over the bill."

He extended his arm. She took it, faintly startled at their comfortable familiarity. She was older now, more sure of herself and what she wanted. She also knew how to get out of difficult situations.

But he seemed calmer too, a lot less upset and a lot less stressed. That attraction she had felt from the moment she met him flowed strong and fine between them.

Maybe she was comfortable because she had thought of him so often, and regretted her part in their strange interaction. Or maybe she was comfortable because she had researched the North family and their company deeply now. She had tried to figure out who they were and what they really did.

Although she hadn't known that Niko was estranged from them.

They walked back to North Wells Street. The streetlights had come on, and the snow flurries reflected in the light. Quite a little storm was brewing. She hadn't expected it.

They discussed the weather and the snow—always safe topics in Chicago—as he led her to DiGillio's, an Italian restaurant that had been part of the city longer than the cigar shop. The entire neighborhood smelled faintly of garlic and tomato sauce.

Her stomach growled. She hadn't realized how hungry she was.

The outdoor tables on the brick-lined patio still had chairs beside them, but the tabletops were covered with wet leaves and a growing blanket of snow.

The plate glass windows on either side of the door contained further reminders of the season. A poster for a Halloween party two days away mentioned a live band. A poster on the other window advertised *Brunch with Santa.* The poster showed a slenderish Santa, handing a present to a pretty little girl with red and green ribbons mixed in her cornrows. A large red sticker beside the poster said, *Brunch With Santa! Get Your Reservations Early! Usually sold out before Thanksgiving!*

Niko pulled open the door. Warm air hit Raine as she stepped inside. The scent of garlic and tomato sauce mixed with baking bread and a faint hint of wood smoke.

It took a moment for her eyes to adjust. The restaurant looked just like it had the last time she had been here, at least ten years before. Tables lined one wall, and doors led to larger rooms behind. The beautiful bar glistened in the evening light. Fake spiderwebs hung off everything, and tiny pumpkins sat in the middle of every table.

It felt odd to see Halloween decorations as the first snow fell. The snowfall had put her in the mood for Christmas, something that almost never happened to her.

"Niiiii-ko!" the bartender shouted, setting down a rag he was holding and coming around the bar. He gave Niko a guy hug, then turned to Raine, eyebrows raised. "What do we have here?"

"Someone I met long ago," Niko said. "Brett DiGillio, meet Raine Wilkins."

The owner. She hadn't expected to see him there on a weekday afternoon.

Raine pulled off her gloves and extended her hand. DiGillio took it. His fingers were vaguely damp, probably from that towel.

He grinned at her, muttered something about it being a pleasure, and then looked at Niko.

"Niko, my man," DiGillio said, "be careful or your lone wolf reputation will fade."

Niko gave a sideways shrug, almost unnoticeable. Raine saw it, but she doubted DiGillio did—or if he did, he ignored it.

"Ms. Wilkins," DiGillio said. "Do you know who you're with?"

"I haven't seen him in—"

"Niko North is the best Santa we have ever had in this city, maybe in this state. We're lucky to get him to work the room for our brunch. Word's gotten around, and the damn thing is the most popular event we host, period. Even if the Cubs or the Sox or Da Bears or Da Bulls are in the playoffs, this place is never as crowded as it is when our Niko dresses up like a jolly old elf."

"Please, Brett," Niko said. "You're not supposed to—"

"And the gifts! Oh, my word," DiGillio said. "We buy them, but they somehow get some of that Niko magic. Because people rave about them years later. The man is gifted, pun intended."

Raine smiled. DiGillio's enthusiasm pleased her rather than putting her off.

"He is," she said. "He gave me these boots years ago and I'm still wearing them."

"It's like he knows the perfect present for each person. He ever leaves, and my holiday season will implode, let me tell you." DiGillio led them to a table near the fireplace. A real fire burned low and warm.

DiGillio pulled out a chair for Raine, then helped her remove her coat. He hung it on a peg nearby. Niko hung his coat beside hers. Both coats dripped on the wood floor.

"Snow, already," Niko said, obviously trying to change the subject.

"Yeah, I'm ready," DiGillio said. "Summer was too hot and too long this year. We can skip the fall crap and move right to winter."

"Looks like we have," Raine said, as she lowered herself into the chair.

"I got some fresh baked garlic bread for you, and a new sauce I want you to try." DiGillio directed that last at Niko. "And you, Santa boy, you keep her around. She's pretty and smart and obviously don't need idiots like us. So watch yourself."

Niko's smile was both warm and dismissive. "I will."

DiGillio scurried off, snapping his fingers as he went, at a woman who lingered near the bar. She picked up the rag and slipped behind the bar, clearly taking over for him.

"Sorry about that," Niko said. "I didn't expect Brett to be here. He usually works the weekends."

"I don't know what you have to apologize about," Raine said. "He likes you."

"Yeah." Niko settled into his chair, moved the napkin-wrapped silverware to one side, and glanced at the fire.

"Does he know your family owns Claus & Company?" she asked.

"No," Niko said, "and I'd like to keep it that way."

"What happened?" she asked. Then she waved her hand as if she could bat the words away. "It's none of my business, sorry. Old habits."

"You're still a reporter?"

"Not like I was," she said. "I freelance now, and blog about various topics."

"And you make enough to live on?" he asked. And then he imitated her hand-waving gesture, and he clearly wasn't making fun of her. He seemed embarrassed. "Sorry. That's none of my business."

She laughed. "Well, maybe we should just be nosy, and have a conversation. What do you say?"

He tilted his head slightly. He had laugh lines—or were they frown lines?—around his eyes. The years had treated him well.

"I think most of our problems that first day came because we weren't nosy, and we didn't ask embarrassing questions," he said. "So yes, I'm all for nosy."

She folded her hands in front of her. "Actually, let's be fair to our younger selves. We didn't have time to ask the right questions. We had no idea what the right questions were. And you were in some kind of crisis."

"Yeah." He nearly whispered the word. As he did, DiGillio arrived at the table. He set a large basket of steaming bread in the center and then gave both Raine and Niko a small bowl filled with a dark red sauce.

"What's this?" Niko asked.

"New family recipe," DiGillio said. "If you like it, it'll be our winter holiday special."

"That's a lot of pressure," Niko said, but he took a spoon and dipped it into the sauce. Then he nodded at Raine. "If I try, you try."

She smiled, dipped her spoon as well, and took a taste. The sauce was rich and beefy, with flavorful tomatoes, oregano, and some spices she couldn't identify. And then, just as she thought the taste was over, some kind of sharp pepper bit the back of her tongue.

"Wow," she said. "That has quite a punch."

"Brett is a master," Niko said. "Serve it with…what? Rigatoni?"

"I was thinking good, old-fashioned spaghetti," Brett said. " You want some of this for dinner? Or I'll make you chicken parm or anything else you want."

He looked at Niko when he said chicken parm, so it was clear Niko ordered that often.

"This sauce with spaghetti would be wonderful," Raine said, "and whatever wine you think would go with it."

DiGillio raised an eyebrow at Niko. "Pretty, smart, and with good taste. Niko—"

"I got it," Niko said, cutting him off. "And I'll have the same thing—without the wine. Just some coffee."

"I got that," DiGillio said. "Like I'd serve you wine."

And he walked away.

Raine tilted her head. "Did I miss something?"

Niko shrugged one shoulder. "Spirits and I...well, my entire family, really...we don't get along."

Her eyes narrowed. Had he been drinking that night she met him? Was that what had been going on?

"And before you ask," he said, "I learned that lesson in what you would call high school."

"What *I* would call high school?" she asked.

"I wasn't raised here," he said.

"You can't tell from your accent," she said with a smile.

He looked startled. "I still have an accent?"

"The kind only the best European boarding schools provide," she said.

He studied her for a moment. "You looked up my history."

She shook her head. Then stopped, frowned, and sighed. "I *tried* to look up your history. Your web presence is pretty tiny. It looks like someone scrubs any reference to the North family continually."

"Yeah," he said. "That doesn't surprise me."

"But you don't know," she said.

He shrugged, then opened both hands in a *whatever* gesture. "I haven't spoken to anyone in my family in years."

"Why not?" she asked, going for the full nosy treatment. "Was it the press conference?"

He grabbed a piece of garlic bread and set it on the bread plate. "That's part of it. But I knew—that night we met—I should have just run away, like I said to you. I wanted to. I had already insulted two patrons at that dance because I wouldn't dance with them, not that I could. I'm still terrible at dancing. I was just honest, which I guess wasn't allowed. I was told to step out of the room so everyone could cool off."

"And you took it literally," she said.

He nodded. "I went outside, saw how pretty it all was, and then saw you. You were perfectly framed in one of the lights

73

from the street. You looked like something out of Hans Christian Andersen. You were so beautiful."

Her cheeks warmed. She hadn't expected that.

"I had this moment," he said. "It was almost like a vision. You and I, running away together, escaping my family and whatever forced you to stand in the snow. I'd made up quite a fantasy by the time we arrived downtown. I was convinced we'd be together. But of course, I didn't tell you. I don't tell people things—I *didn't* tell people things. I just lived these movies in my head, and that's bad, as my therapist says."

"Therapist?" she asked. Most people didn't admit they were in therapy, particularly over a first dinner.

But then, he'd just confessed to alcoholics in the family and to a dangerously overactive imagination. In those instances, a therapist sounded like a necessity.

"Yeah," he said. "Eight years and counting. I'm a lot less impulsive, a lot more thoughtful, and I try to communicate."

He flashed her an awkward smile.

"It was you, really, who started it," he said.

"Started what?" she asked.

"My quest for self-improvement. You were honest with me that night. You said that I scared you or startled you or alarmed you or however you phrased it, and that my behavior wasn't appropriate, and I thought it was. So I started asking people about appropriate behavior. Asking isn't appropriate, either, but I'm just not good at reading people's reactions, which is— well. You don't need my full psychological history. You asked about my family."

"I did," she said. She was a bit surprised at herself. She wasn't alarmed by his admissions or his rambling. Maybe she was older. Or maybe she had learned to read people better herself.

The female bartender, a lot less intrusive than DiGillio, brought a gigantic mug filled with coffee for Niko and a glass of red wine for Raine. Raine picked up the glass, swirled it, sniffed, and smiled with approval. A cabernet. Perfect.

Niko waited until the bartender left, then he held one hand over the steaming coffee, as if he were cold.

"Claus & Company shut down the Uplift Fund right after the press conference. They didn't even do a token attempt at keeping it alive. I had spent five years setting up the fund, and because I screwed up one thing—the thing they think is the most important, mind you, but one thing—they destroyed all of my work."

He shrugged. This one was a noncommittal, I-really-don't-care shrug. But he did. His tone said he did.

Raine took a sip of the wine. It was rich and full. She kept her gaze on Niko's, afraid that if she stopped looking directly at him, and nodding at the appropriate places, he would stop talking.

"They had a sleigh ready for me right after I spoke to you, and they were going to send me directly to the toy factory. I'd've been packing toys and dealing with fritzing computer systems that weren't compatible with—um, with the systems that Claus & Company had. I went back, but I walked into that factory, and I couldn't stay. I just couldn't."

He pulled the bread apart, then dunked one of the pieces in the spaghetti sauce.

"And that's when I really did run away," he said.

She had a lot of questions, but she didn't want to ask them all, afraid that he would stop telling her anything. But she held them in her mind, particularly his weird reference to a sleigh. Had he misspoken?

If she asked about the sleigh, she would be ignoring the emotional context of the conversation. She had to say something, and it had to be the right something.

"So you came back here?" she asked.

He shook his head. "I went to England for a while, then

decided I needed a real education. I finished my undergraduate degree in social work, then got a masters in non-profit management from the University of Minnesota."

"I didn't even know there was such a field of study," she said.

"There is, and it's pretty valuable. You learn fund-raising and money management, and all that stuff I was just guessing at when I was setting up the Uplift Fund the first time. I was trying to piggy-back off of what Claus & Company had been doing for nearly a century, but that's not the same as setting it all up yourself."

"I guess not," she said. "Then what? You had an apprentice-ship or something?"

"For me, yes," he said. "I wanted to learn. Then last year, I came back here. I started the Uplift Foundation, and while it's not growing as fast as I'd like, it's growing faster than most. If I had the clout that Claus & Company has, I'd raise a lot more money, but now I worry that had I done that all those years ago, too much of the money would have gone to the wrong things. You reporters were right to ask about administration and management, and I'm afraid my answers wouldn't have been as good as I thought they were at the time."

Raine grabbed a piece of garlic bread. The butter oozed off it onto her skin. She set the piece on her bread plate and licked her fingers, then blushed at her rudeness.

He watched, clearly amused.

"What about you?" he asked. "You left Chicago?"

"Before the collapse of the *Chicago Courier*," she said. "I've worked all over the country, but I finally decided to come home."

"And you blog," he said.

She nodded.

"About what?" he asked.

She let out a small sigh. Here was where she might lose him.

"I normally don't tell people what I blog about. I do it anonymously."

She paused, not sure what she was hoping for. Did she want him to ask about her blog or did she want him to change the subject back to himself?

"So, you can't tell me," he said.

"Well," she said. "You sort of inspired the blog. Something you said at the press conference."

"Something *I* said?" he asked.

She nodded. Then she took a deep breath. She had promised him that they could be nosy, and he was asking all the right questions. She had to answer them if she wanted to see him again.

Did she want to see him again?

She barely thought of the question before she knew the answer. Of course, she wanted to see him again. She had wanted to see him again ever since they parted—and he took a sleigh back to company headquarters, whatever that meant.

"I write a blog called *Fiefdoms and Fairy Tales*," she said.

He let out a half laugh, then tilted his head back. For a minute, she thought he was going to get out of his chair and leave. Then he started to laugh.

"Holy…." He still didn't swear, but he didn't substitute stupid words either. "*You're* Fiefdoms and Fairy Tales?"

"I'm afraid so," she said.

"You are a thorn in the side of Claus & Company. They *hate* you."

"I know," she said, wondering how he knew if he wasn't in touch with them.

"And you did that exposé of the Archetype Place. It was brilliant, even if it didn't go far enough. And the thing about the strange goings-on around Quixotic, that restaurant in Portland? It would've been even better if you hadn't mentioned the TV show *Grimm*."

"Too obvious," she said, feeling both pleased and uncomfortable. "If I hadn't made the connection, my readers would have. The TV show had a little too much in common with some of the things happening at that restaurant."

"You're close, you know?" Niko said. "You're..."

His voice trailed off. Then he shook his head and ran a hand over his face.

"And this is why no one ever wants me to talk to the press," he said, more to himself than to her.

She waited for him to continue, but he didn't. So, she said, "You know, if I was still working for the *Chicago Courier*, I'd ask you to elaborate on that."

He looked down and shook his head.

"But I'm not going to," she said, "because we're catching up. Or introducing ourselves. Or whatever you want to call this."

At that moment, DiGillio swept out of the kitchen with two plates on his hands. He set the plates before them with a flourish.

"*Buon appetito!*" he said, then bowed a little, and walked away.

The food smelled heavenly. Raine hadn't realized just how hungry she was.

Niko looked at the plate like it was covered with pine boughs. Then he glanced up at her.

"You said I inspired your blog," he said, almost reluctantly. "What do you mean?"

"The title, for one thing," she said. "You mentioned fairy tales, and you said Claus & Company was a fiefdom."

"I did?" he asked.

"At the press conference," she said, picking up her fork.

"Of course I did," he said, sighing.

"I wrote a long series of articles on Claus & Company, but I could never penetrate the layers of corporate structure. No one could. The newspaper finally pulled me off the story and moved me to something else, but by then, I had moved to the business section of the paper. And then I got hired away by some Internet start-ups, and kept writing about the intersection between entertainment and business, and that led to my blog, which I admit, is a lot more fanciful than the stuff I wrote for the papers, but just as well researched."

"I'm amazed you found anything," he said.

"If you know how to dig, everything is on the Internet," she said, then paused with her fork above the plate. "Except you."

"Yeah," he said. "If you don't want to be found, you don't participate. I only just started with all that social media stuff, and I did it under the name Uplift Foundation, not as Niko North."

"So, let's get some of the other nosy stuff out of the way." She didn't want to talk about the blog any more. And she wanted to know a few things. She hoped she sounded flip. "Married? Kids?"

"No, and no," he said. "Sadly. I like kids. Never met anyone who caught my attention like y—well, I never really met anyone, although I did date a lot at university. And you?"

"No to both," she said. "It never worked out."

They were quiet for moment. Raine used that silence to dig in to the pasta. The sauce was even better on al dente spaghetti. Or maybe it was the mix of flavors with the wine.

Niko ate a bite as well, then smiled. Apparently, the food was to his liking after all.

"All right then," he said after a moment, "back to my rude question. You make enough blogging and freelancing?"

"Yeah," she said. "A lot more than I made as a reporter. And how about you?"

"I'm still part of the family, whether I want to be or not. I have a trust. I live off the interest. In an attempt to get me to go home, they tried to cut off my money, but they couldn't. Once my family gives a gift, they can't take it back."

That mention of family and gift-giving again. She decided not to pursue it at the moment. Instead, she made light.

"So I can't give you the boots back?" she asked.

He grinned. "Nope. You're stuck with them."

She laughed.

"Anyway," he said, "I don't take any money from the fund, not even in administrative costs. That's my donation. I'm still setting up, but my partners and I, we're actually funding a few things around the city."

"Do you need promotion for the things you're doing?" she asked. She could write some freelance articles. She was already envisioning the pitch—the Redemption of Niko North (or the Revival of a Really Good Idea).

"Not yet," Niko said. "There're too many charities clamoring for attention during the holiday season. I don't want to be one."

"But some of that is for tax purposes," she said. "Get your donations in by the end of December for the tax year, and all of that."

"Yeah." And she could tell from his tone what he thought of people who had to be incentivized to give to charity. "We'll think about that when we're established. Our big push will be in the spring. We're coming up with slogans now, and packages, and methods of giving."

"Still focused on children?" she asked.

"Homelessness and hunger," he said. "The bane of our very rich culture."

She nodded. Then decided to say, "I was homeless as a kid."

He looked up, clearly startled. "For how long?"

"High school," she said. "And some of middle school."

"But you went to Northwestern." Ah, so he had checked up on her too.

"I did," she said. "Scholarship."

"How did you study? How did you manage? What—"

She held up her fork to stop him. "I'll tell you, but not over such a nice dinner. I'd rather not relive those years if I can avoid it."

He nodded a bit too quickly. "I understand. But you can tell that this is a passion of mine, and to meet a success, to realize I know a success, that helps more than you can imagine."

She felt warm. Maybe it was the wine or the sauce or the fire. Or maybe it was the regard of the man sitting across from her.

"Put that way," she said, "I'd be…well, not happy to tell you. But willing. My dad lost his job, and then my parents couldn't make payments on their house, and by the time they figured out what to do, my mom couldn't find paying work, either, and the house got foreclosed on, and then no one would rent to us, and suddenly, we were living in our car."

"House directly to car?" he asked.

"With some hotel rooms along the way," she said.

"Incurring credit card debt," he said.

She nodded. "It followed them forever. We went from shelter to shelter, and let me tell you, there are more badly run shelters than good ones. They can be scary places."

"I'd like to know what you think makes one run well. And what we can do to improve. Can you consult with us, Raine?" He was leaning forward, hands clasped, staring at her so intently she could feel his gaze as clearly as if he touched her.

Then his right eye twinkled, just like it had at the press conference.

He flushed, put a hand over his eye, and said, "Sorry. I usually know—I mean, I can usually prevent—Sorry."

She frowned. "What was that?"

He shook his head. "It's just weird. It's a family thing. It's—"

"Niko, we decided we'd be honest." She said.

"You wouldn't believe it," he said.

"Try me," she said.

He stirred the spaghetti on his plate. "I like you."

"I like you," she said. "But that doesn't have anything to do with this."

"It has everything to do with it," he said. He sighed. "I didn't buy your boots."

Her stomach clenched over the spaghetti. He *stole* the boots? And she'd worn them for years.

"Well," he said, still stirring. "That's not entirely accurate. I bought boots for you. And then I made them into the perfect boots."

He looked up. His eyes were blue and clear and seemed to have added radiance. His face was so bright and perfect that it looked like a painting of a handsome man's face.

With both hands, he tucked his hair behind his ears. They had a slight point.

"You *made* the boots?" she repeated.

He nodded, looking a little frightened. "Just like I do at the Santa brunch. You heard Brett. The gifts are always spot-on."

"'The perfect present for each person,'" she said, quoting DiGillio. "He called it 'Niko magic.'"

"Yeah," Niko said softly. "Brett sees things clearer than he probably should."

"You're telling me that you have magic." She laughed, but the laugh sounded nervous, even to her ears. "You went home in a sleigh after the press conference, and you have magic, and you're the best Santa your friend has ever hired. I'd think you were pranking me, but you had no idea we were going to meet up today. Unless you do this to anyone whom you bring here."

Niko bit his bottom lip. "I'm not pranking you, Raine."

"You're a family member at Claus & Company," she said, "the organization that handles Santa's image worldwide. You said that your family does things fast. How fast, Niko?"

He sighed. Then he shook his head.

"Niko," she said, urging him to answer.

"You saw what they did to me," he said. "And how fast."

She frowned. She'd seen a lot of strange things over the years. That was why she blogged about it all. But because she'd seen strange things, she sometimes leapt to the wrong conclusion.

An embarrassing conclusion.

However, because she had decided on full honesty with Niko, she asked the question she normally would have held back.

"You want me to believe you're Santa Claus?" she asked.

"No," he said quickly.

"Okay, then," she said, "you're in line to become Santa Claus."

"No," he said. Then sighed again. "Not anymore."

His words hung between them.

She could walk away, she could continue to ask questions, or she could pretend this conversation never happened. She wasn't about to leave, and she wasn't good at pretending.

"You're not in line because you ran away," she said.

"I don't want the job," he said. "My siblings do. They're still fighting over it."

"So, the magic—they let you keep it?" she asked.

He shook his head again. "That's not how it works. I was born with it, Raine. I'm an S-Elf."

"A *what?*" Somehow believing that he was an elf was harder than believing he had magic.

"An S-Elf." Niko shrugged. This time, the shrug was apologetic. "From Santa's line. There are a lot of us, because there've been a lot of Santas over the centuries. Or St. Nicks, or whatever you want to call us. Many cultures use different phrases. I'm part of the current line. My father is—"

"Santa Claus?" she asked. Her heart was beating hard. Seriously? Did Niko really expect her to believe that?

His nod was so small she almost didn't see it.

She was beginning to get mad. She hated it when people made fun of her. "So S-Elves are what? Not human, right?"

"I don't know how to answer that," he said. "We're human enough. I mean, most S-Elves marry humans. The mix doesn't seem to cause harm, and might even augment the S-Elf magic."

"S-Elf magic." She was being sarcastic, but she couldn't help herself. "And what is that, exactly?"

"The perfect gift," he said. "The ability to make the sleighs run. A surfeit of magic, if used in the service of others. And so many other things."

She let out a small laugh. "So, Santa's real, but he ignores poor kids and kids from other religions, and he could solve poverty but won't and magic is real, but it's only for consumerism, and Claus & Company—"

"No, no." Niko held his hands up. "When all this started, the world was smaller. Or what we knew of the world was smaller. Claus & Company really was a Northern European thing."

"Which makes it so much better." She wasn't sure if she was responding to the illogic of it all or to the fact that she had had so many awful Christmases after her family lost their home or to the fact that so many other kids were just like her.

"If my family could do away with poverty, they would," he said. "They're working hard on trying to reach out to the poor. That's what the charities are all about. And there's an entire religious wing of Claus & Company that tries to help kids of religions where there is no Christmas tradition, but that's harder, because no one wants to co-opt someone else's beliefs—"

"And that makes it all better?" she snapped. "Your family has magic and billions and it can't repair the world?"

"No," he said quietly. "It can't."

The sadness in his tone actually stopped her. She let out a breath. Made herself breathe. Made herself *think*.

"That's what the Uplift Fund was about," she said.

"Yes," he said. "I was going to move the family's focus from presents to good works. My uncle managed to do some of that —those toy drives of the 1990s, the food donations of recent years, the emphasis on children's charities at the holiday season —but it was all patchwork. I wanted to do something so much bigger."

"And they stopped you?" She couldn't quite believe she was asking the question. Did that mean part of her thought he was telling the truth?

He ran a hand over his mouth, almost hiding another sad smile. "To answer that, I'd have to defend Claus & Company, and I don't want to."

"Do it anyway," she said. "Make me understand."

"The image. They have become focused on the image. It makes sense; it brings in money that they then use for materials for the non-magical toys. It keeps the troops fed. It enables the existing charities to work."

"And you screwed up the image?" she asked.

"They thought I would. I came close. I would have had to go back to training as well as work in the toy factory," he said. "I'd already gone through the courses at Image Consulting, and they said I was hopeless. They were right."

"Toy factory," she said. "Training. Home. And a sleigh. Don't tell me. You're from the North Pole."

The hand moved from his mouth to his forehead. "Not your North Pole," he mumbled.

"Excuse me?" she asked.

He shook his head. "I'm not supposed to do this."

"Do what?" she asked.

"Tell anyone—ah, hell." He stood up and walked to her side of the table. Then he crouched. "I don't have good social skills, Raine. At home, they say I was born without social skills, whatever that means. And so, here, listen, if I offend you, I'm sorry. But I have to know something."

Her heart was still beating hard. She now understood why her younger self had run away from him. Her younger self hadn't learned how to differentiate between people without social skills and people who were dangerous.

She knew the difference now. And even though he was too close to her—or so her younger self would have said—she didn't mind, as crazy as all of his talk was.

She really didn't mind.

He took her hand. That electricity remained. She liked his touch.

"May I kiss you?" he asked. "It'll probably be my only chance ever, given how badly I'm screwing up yet again, but I would really like to—"

She leaned forward and pressed her lips against his. His mouth was slightly open and he sighed into her before deepening the kiss. He didn't taste of spaghetti, like she expected. He tasted of hot chocolate, and a little deeper into the kiss, of peppermint.

She put her hands on his shoulders and pulled him even closer. They stood together, and the kiss became more than a kiss. It became—

"Get a room," DiGillio said from behind her. "After you finish the lovely dinner I prepared for you. Or, I can move everything to one of the back rooms and ask that you not be disturbed."

Raine pulled back from Niko. His face was flushed—hers probably was too—and his eyes looked like tiny fireworks were going off behind the lenses. He bowed his head, put his hand over his eyes, and then looked up again. The sparkling was gone—and its disappearance actually made her feel sad.

Niko blinked, then looked over her shoulder at DiGillio. "We don't need a room. Sorry to upend things around here—"

"Stop apologizing," Raine said. Her friend Verity would have been shocked that Raine had even said that. Verity

86

would've been even more shocked at what Raine said next. "There's no one else here. What's the problem?"

DiGillio's expression was cold. "He's my friend. And I heard part of the conversation. I don't want you to hurt him. He's fragile."

"I am not," Niko said.

"You are," DiGillio said. "You're naïve and wonderful, and sometimes we cynics got to run interference for innocent souls like yours. And I'm going to do that. So, unless you're serious about him, lady, back off. Because Niko has only two speeds. Charmingly casual or deeply involved."

"You've seen that before," Raine said, beginning to understand.

"He's a good man doing good works, and you're not going to screw him up. I mean it. The last time he got hurt, he was down for weeks."

She glanced at Niko. He shrugged—an I-don't-know-what-he's-talking-about shrug. Then he returned to his chair, turned sideways, and faced the fire.

"He's the nicest person I know," DiGillio said.

"I got that," Raine said. "I promise. I won't hurt him. Now, can we finish our conversation?"

DiGillio glanced at Niko. Niko didn't look at him.

"You be careful," DiGillio said to both of them. Then, as he walked back to the bar, he added, "I won't listen, but if things get heated—"

"I can handle it, Brett," Niko said, loudly enough to be heard. "I promise."

Raine sat down. She waited for Niko to say something, but he didn't. So, after about five minutes, she said, "You said you had to know something. Then you asked if you could kiss me. Was that what you needed to know?"

"No." Niko was still staring at the fire. "I had to know if the conversation we would have next was worth the risk."

"What conversation?" she asked.

He turned his chair and faced her. Then he moved the plate of food away from him, which probably caused DiGillio distress.

Niko leaned forward. "If I tell you things, there's no going back, Raine. And you're a blogger, so you might use this stuff, or say negative things about me."

She started to protest, but he held up his hand.

"You're a blogger," he said again. "That means you have no magic. Which means—"

"What?" she asked.

"Technology. It doesn't work around the magical. It always falls apart or fails or—"

"You mean, as in, I have to replace my computer every year or the fact that my smart phone glitches? Have you thought about the fact that I'm not driving much?" She sounded defensive. She *was* defensive, in a weird way. She wasn't sure why, though. Maybe it was his tone.

He blinked. "You have tech issues?"

"Since I had to start using it regularly. Yes. I do. It's annoying. What does that mean?"

He smiled. His smile was large. "That makes sense. That's how you saw into the Archetype Place."

"What?" she asked.

"Most regular people can't even find it, and you managed to get inside." His grin grew. "That's great news."

It hadn't been when she went inside the Archetype Place. Everyone had worked hard to get her out of the building as fast as possible.

"What's great news?" she asked.

"You have magic. I should've seen it."

She felt exasperated. He couldn't distract her like that. "The conversation," she reminded him.

He nodded, his smile fading. "You're on an edge, Raine.

You've skirted it for a long time. It's a place not a lot of people go. It's between the Greater World and my family's world, and that's where—"

"The Greater World," she said. "You mentioned it after the press conference. And you called your family's business 'a little fiefdom in a vast fairy tale.'"

He started. "I did?"

She nodded. "That got me looking—that's the title of my blog. So what are you trying to tell me, Niko? That fairy tales are real?"

"Yes," he said.

She was about to go on when she realized what he said. "Like Santa is real?"

"Yes," he said.

"Exactly like the stories?" she asked.

"Oh, no," he said. "Very different and much more complicated. But there's magic and history and all kinds of things…."

His voice trailed off. Clearly, her disbelief showed on her face.

"I knew you'd think I'm crazy," he said. "Everyone does. I could take you to the North Pole—my family's North Pole— but that would cause me issues, and I can't do that, Raine. I'm not going back there."

"I don't know how this relates to the kiss," she said.

His smile was sad. "I wouldn't have told you any of this if the attraction was only passing."

"One kiss told you it was more than that?" she asked.

"Didn't it tell you?" he asked.

She let out a breath. It had. She had never felt that way before. That single kiss was enough to show her just how deep this relationship could become.

Except that he was crazy.

Except that he probably wasn't.

All those things she'd seen in Los Angeles, all that she had written about in D.C., all the strange phenomena she'd investigated over the years—true?

She wanted them to be.

But she had wanted a great Christmas when she was a kid, too. One of the sad facts of growing up was to let go of childish things.

She waved a hand at DiGillio.

"Can you bring me a to-go box?" she asked.

He nodded, then glanced at Niko. Niko was looking down.

DiGillio went into the kitchen.

"So you're leaving," Niko said.

"I'm thinking," she said. "Is there something I could read, something I could use to verify—"

"No," Niko said.

DiGillio brought back the to-go box, and scraped the spaghetti inside it. He waved the garlic bread as if asking her if she wanted any.

She shook her head.

"I'm paying for dinner," she said. "How much do I owe?"

"On the house," DiGillio said.

"I can't. I owe Niko a dinner," she said.

"On the house," DiGillio said, then glanced at the door. He wanted her out of here. She wanted out too, but she wasn't sure why.

She felt overwhelmed.

She stood, put on her damp coat, and then grabbed the box. She started, "I just need—"

"It's all right," Niko said. "I understand."

But he didn't look at her.

She waited for a moment, and he still didn't look. So she left.

The wet snow had frozen onto the pavement. The sidewalk crunched beneath her feet. The walk home would be treacherous, and she knew she wasn't going to pay attention.

So she walked the half block to the Sedgwick Station and took the L home. By the time she got there, she felt as bad as she had the night she met Niko.

What was wrong with her? Why did she always feel like she needed to walk away from that man? And why did she feel guilty afterwards?

She let out a breath as she removed the boots.

Because she believed him. Because she believed in fairy tales. Because she believed in magic.

And she wanted to be rational enough not to.

CHAPTER 7

*S*HE SPENT THE next month researching and digging and searching and blogging about small things while looking into the big thing.

The big thing was magic and fairy tales and Claus & Company. The big thing was that kiss, which she couldn't get out of her mind. The big thing was that pair of boots, which she looked up on the Internet and found that there were no other boots like them anywhere—not on eBay, not on Craig's List, not on someone's Pinterest page.

The boots were unique, they had no wear-and-tear, and they still fit, after years and years and years.

They were hers, and no one else's. No one else had a pair like that.

The perfect boots.

She also researched the Uplift Foundation. She had no trouble finding its non-profit documents, its tax records, its backers, and its financial situation. Everything was as Niko said: He didn't take a salary and he paid for the overhead out of his own pocket. He'd had to get some kind of legal exemption to do that, but he had, and it would all live beyond him.

The other backers were names she recognized, many of whom were very active in Chicago charities, others active nationwide. The fund had already established a bridge program for needy kids so that they would get meals when school was not in session. There were plans on the drawing board for a new kind of shelter (still under discussion) and ways to keep children in dangerous neighborhoods safe after school and on weekends.

There was very little promotional material about the Uplift Foundation. It sounded like a need-to-know organization. But it did have a website and a mission statement: To provide opportunities for every single child in the Greater Chicago area, no matter what the child's circumstances, no matter what the challenges.

She loved that mission. She loved that dream.

And after she had done her research, after she understood that people with both millions of dollars and private detectives on the payroll believed in Niko enough to give him cash to run his organization, she realized that she was being too judgmental.

Niko believed in magic and fairy tales and Santa Claus. If he saw himself as part of a great lineage of fairy tale creatures, so what? It didn't matter. Maybe those were the things that he told himself to get by at night, to make it through the days.

She had told herself a lot of untrue things to survive her childhood. And she liked peering around the edges, just like she had that day she met him—not just staring at the rich, but believing that sometimes even the most mundane events could produce just a bit of magic.

That dance at that mansion in Lincoln Park had produced magic. It had conjured Niko North and inserted him into her life.

He was a good man. She knew it; she could sense it. And even if she didn't trust her instincts (and she clearly didn't), other people believed the same thing. Enough to support him on a crazy project that even if he had had the backing of Claus & Company, it would still take a miracle to pull off—at least, on as large a scale as he wanted to.

She had taken a lot of risks in her life, but the one risk she had never taken, the one risk she had been unwilling to take, was with her heart.

It was time. Actually, it was past time.

She hoped he would give her one last chance.

CHAPTER 8

*S*HE COULD HEAR the laughter from a block away. Despite the cold, the doors to DiGillio's were open, and the laughter from inside had spilled into the neighborhood like the warmth was spilling onto the patio.

The restaurant was clearly past capacity and no one seemed to care. Somehow she managed to squeeze past the parents clutching their flocks of children, the grandparents looking on, and the restaurant staff dressed like Santa's elves.

She found a place to stand near the back. She climbed on a chair and leaned against the wall. From her perch, she could see the gigantic Christmas tree near the fireplace. The most amazing Santa stood in front of it, holding a toddler above his head. The toddler, a little boy, was squealing with laughter. Santa twirled him and then set him down.

The boy ran off, holding a gift that Raine hadn't seen Santa give him. A young mother scooped the boy up, asking him what he got. His answer was lost in the general din, but his look of pleasure was not.

All of the children here looked happy. So did the parents. So did the restaurant staff.

And Santa—fat and jolly and shaking like a bowl full of jelly —appeared to be having the time of his life.

The air around him sparkled, and more than once she'd seen an amazing twinkle flash from his eyes.

She watched in silence as the holiday brunch ended, with candy canes for everyone and a mighty ho-ho-ho from Santa himself.

DiGillio—the ugliest elf she had ever seen—somehow managed to get the guests out of the restaurant. They left laughing, exclaiming about the experience, comparing notes, and comparing presents.

She climbed down off the chair, using the wall to brace herself. Then she felt a hand at her back.

Santa stood behind her, helping her stay balanced. Up close, his youth was apparent. His eyes were a deep blue, and he looked a little unsure of himself.

She was unsure of herself, too. She wasn't sure how to talk to him.

"Brett is right," she said. "You're the best Santa I've ever seen."

Niko smiled—his smile, not the bow-lipped Santa smile. "Thank you."

He paused, as if he were waiting for something. Probably her apology.

"I—." She stopped herself. "I, um, want to say that I'm sorry…"

He put a gloved finger over her lips. "No. No apologies. Just a question."

At first, she thought he meant she could ask him a question, but his finger remained.

"Do you believe in love at first sight?" he asked.

She took a deep breath. She would have to step away from him to answer, or pull his hand aside or something.

"Because I do," he said. "That's real magic. You look at

someone, say, across a snowy yard, and you know, you just know, that person was waiting for you."

She ducked her head to one side. She couldn't help herself. She was a reporter and a realist. "Love's a pretty big word," she said.

"Yes," he said. "It is."

She stared at him. He tugged on the beard, and it came off as if nothing had held it in place. But she knew dozens of little hands had tugged on it too, and in those instances, it had stayed on.

"Do you believe in it?" he asked.

"Love at first sight?" She thought for a second. Attraction, maybe. But that moment when he appeared behind her, wearing a tuxedo and looking like something out of her dreams, that was the moment she'd thought of instantly when he had asked the question.

"It's like magic, isn't it? Love?" he asked, unable or unwilling to wait for her answer. "You don't believe in it until it happens to you."

She smiled at him. "Magic's a big word too."

He shrugged one red-clad shoulder. "There was a lot of magic here today."

"And happy children," she said.

He nodded.

She could ignore his questions. She could take this one hour at a time, rather like she'd planned when she got here. But she had been thinking about risk—and taking risks.

"I think there are different kinds of magic, like there are different kinds of love," she said. "I think what you did here today, that was magic."

He froze, like he had that day of the press conference.

"But I also think that getting people to support a new charity, one you really believe in, is a kind of magic. Just like breaking away from an old system, one you don't believe in, takes a kind of courage that most people never have."

He let out a breath.

"I'm really cautious about some things," she said. "My heart. I don't know if I believe in love at first sight."

He looked down, and then away, like he had that day a few weeks ago, the day she had walked out on him again.

"But I believe that the world gives you second and third chances to fall for the right person," she said. "This is my third chance."

His head snapped toward hers. It was so odd to see his handsome face beneath a shock of white hair. She knew she was seeing his future. One day, he would look like Santa Claus, whether he was or not.

"And?" he asked.

"And," she said, "I'm going to take it, if you're still willing."

"Willing to what?" he asked.

"Show me magic," she said. "Let me help you build the Uplift Foundation. Kiss me again."

He grinned. "I can do those things."

She raised her eyebrows at him.

He let out a small laugh, then leaned forward, hands around her waist, pulling her close despite the fake belly. He kissed her. His flavor, the same as before, chocolate and peppermint, and something else, something so him she wondered how she had lived without it.

Maybe she didn't believe in love at first sight. Maybe she needed evidence of magic.

But this, this moment, it was going a long way to convincing her.

He broke the kiss, and leaned his forehead against hers. "I've never met anyone quite like you," he said softly.

She smiled. "Is that a good thing?"

"Oh, yes," he said.

"I've never met anyone like you either," she said, and then she kissed him again.

She was falling in love. She could feel it. Just like she felt magic around her. It didn't matter if it was true magic or just the magic of the holiday.

But it was real to her.

And to him.

This time, she broke the kiss. "I can help you. With the Uplift Foundation, with promotion—"

"Later." His lips brushed hers. "We'll think about all of that later."

"What are we going to think about now?" she asked playfully.

"Nothing," he said, "Except…"

He leaned away from her and looked at DiGillio.

"Got a room?" Niko asked him.

DiGillio laughed. "I thought you would never ask."

He pointed to a door near the Christmas tree. Niko wrapped Raine in his arms and half-led her, half-carried her to the back.

Once inside the room, he closed the door, and peeled off the top of his fat suit. He was perfectly proportioned. He put his arms around her, and pulled her close.

"Christmas magic," he said softly.

She laughed. "Show me how it works," she said.

And so he did.

KRISTINE GRAYSON

"Kristine Grayson has carved out her own special and unique place in the romance genre."
—RT Book Reviews

Tidings of Comfort and Joy

THE SANTA SERIES

Read more in the Santa Series with *Tidings of Comfort and Joy*, available from your favorite bookseller. Following is a sample chapter from that book.

TIDINGS OF COMFORT AND JOY

THE GODDESS OF ALL MACHINES

TIDINGS OF COMFORT AND JOY
SAMPLE CHAPTER

The first thing Dallas Demaris would have told anyone who asked was that she loved the office building. Really, really loved it. Set on a cliff overlooking the ocean in Malibu, California, the office building had everything she had ever wanted in a work space. It had:

•Floor-to-ceiling windows everywhere, to soak in the sunlight and maximize the views.

•The view, which was of:

The ocean—and not some gray, scary, violent, *cold* ocean, but the ocean the way it should look, all blue and sparkly and inviting.

The sky—which was generally blue and sparkly and inviting as well.

The beach—which was pristine (except where it wasn't), and if she squinted just a bit (past the ships and the outlines of oil rigs) she could almost imagine the world as it once was, all pretty and ready…to be ruined by human beings.

•A soft carpet, which enabled her to stand and look at the view for a long period of time.

In truth, the office was beautifully designed, with workspaces that flowed. Each workspace had its windows. Even the corridors had views. Whenever she stepped off the elevator (which, sadly, did not have views), she was greeted by a bank of windows, revealing some part of the Southern California coastline.

The entire working part of the building faced westward. The rest of the building was built into that cliff face, and the storage parts of the building were the ones on the cliff-face side.

Presciently, the building was made of concrete so even when the scary wildfires scraped across Malibu—and they did, far too often for her taste—the office would survive or would *have* survived, even if it hadn't had magical protection, which it did.

It also had been retrofitted for earthquake protection, by the mortals who were following mortal law, which simply made the building safer through a non-magical event. The building had always been protected against a real earthquake, but mortals didn't recognize magical protections, hence the retrofitting.

Mortals also didn't realize what this building was, and that was by design. Most people saw a rectangular gray and glass building rising out of the cliff face, thinking the office was just another wealthy person's home or big company's monument to excess, instead of a working office, filled with mostly disgruntled employees who, for some odd reason, would rather have been elsewhere.

Dallas didn't want to be anywhere else for any reason. She loved the warmth. She loved the sunshine. She loved the beach, the ocean, and even those tinder-dry mountains behind that cliff.

She had been lucky enough to score (an exceedingly expensive) rental nearby, but even back in the days when she had to drive to work, she didn't mind the traffic in the greater Los

Angeles area. She figured it and the smog and the congestion were a small price to pay for getting to work in one of the prettiest places she had ever seen.

The second thing Dallas would have told anyone who asked (and really, no one ever did) was that she loved the work. She'd been doing it for nearly two hundred years now, trying to make machines compatible with magic, and when that didn't work, inventing machines that were. She had a knack for making devices bow to her whims.

It had taken her a greater part of the last century to figure out how to make magic and computers compatible, but she had done the deed well enough that most of the magical could now carry cell phones without having them explode on a daily basis.

Sure, she wasn't able to make magic and tech completely compatible—not mortal non-magical tech—but she could invent tech that had magic as its base.

Her brain was filled with fiddly little details of all kinds of science and magical history, waiting for each fiddly little detail to serve its purpose in the grander scheme of things. She wasn't sure what that grand scheme was, but she knew—deep down—that she was part of that grand scheme.

And one day, she would figure out how, exactly, she fit in.

But—and anyone who was paying attention would know that there was a *but* coming, wouldn't they?—her job wasn't ideal. She was the only woman who worked in the office, not because she was the only woman who could combine tech with magic, but because she was the only woman who had actually bullied her way into this place.

Or rather, obliviously barged her way in. Because Dallas obliviously barged her way into a lot of success over the centuries. She simply didn't take no for an answer. She also refused to believe that her brain was inferior to anyone else's— man, woman, transgender, standard magical creature, nonstandard magical creature, or something brand-spankin' new.

And since she took that attitude toward life, she figured most of the pushback she got on the things she did was because she was brilliant and ahead of the curve, rather than because she was a woman.

Although today, standing inside the corporate meeting room of the office, it was hard to ignore the fact that she was being chosen for this new job not because she was the best person for the job, but because she was a woman—or rather *the* woman—and the men who ran the place wanted her the hell out of here.

The men who ran the place had been in charge for a Very Long Time. Before the office was built into this cliff face sometime in the last century. Those men—and there were a dozen of them—weren't in Malibu because they loved it. They still considered Malibu a backwater of the first order, since all but two of them were European.

In truth, they couldn't get more out of touch. The director, Waldo Ranklesworth, flew home to England every evening. Literally flew. He didn't like to spend any more time in the Colonies, as he put it, than he had to.

Ranklesworth was round. His face was round, his torso was round, and his stubby little legs were round(ish). He had had a mustache since the nineteenth century, and it had finally turned white to match his thick head of hair. That mustache had either dug deep grooves into his jowls or had forced his skin into jowls—Dallas couldn't really tell. His bushy eyebrows sometimes brushed against his eyelashes, creating a tangle that he had to rub away like a child rubbing sleep out of his eyes.

Dallas had had trouble taking Ranklesworth seriously from the moment she met him. His pinched tone and his accent, liberally borrowed *from* Oxford but not *of* Oxford, didn't help.

He tended to hire men similar to him, following the mandate of the company, which was that most Western languages and cultures be represented. He wouldn't have been able to handle the office if it had to handle Asian cultures, African cultures, and Middle Eastern cultures. He had been heard to argue that the Eastern European cultures weren't really European at all.

If Dallas were militant—and she wasn't, not really, because it interfered with her work—she would have been some kind of whistleblower. Although she was never entirely sure who Ranklesworth actually worked for, or what the hierarchy of the office was once you got outside of this particular building.

Dallas had always been happy to do the almost-impossible assignments the men around the table had given her, because she liked a challenge. When she first started here, before there were even roads heading to the beach, she had believed the men gave her the biggest challenges because she had the biggest brain.

Slowly, she realized, they had given her the biggest challenges because they couldn't figure out any other way to get rid of her.

And really, it was the other men at the table who had taught her that. Not the ten Ranklesworth clones, who all had varying degrees of roundness, mustachedness, and thick-white-hairedness, but the rotating seats of the two Americans.

At first, those two men were also round and mustachioed and white-haired (one illegitimately, using magic to make his bald pate look just like Ranklesworth's head). Those two men had both come from the East Coast, from "good" families, and got tired of Ranklesworth's snobbery, moving on and up, as the men liked to say.

But then orders came from on high for some diversity in the office, and that at first meant men from the Middle West and California itself, not that it worked out for them either. And then the 1960s happened, and diversity took on a new meaning, and so did the levels of passive-aggressive viciousness. The two American seats usually went to a man of color, who would get angry at The Way Things Were Done, and would usually try to recruit Dallas to help foment some rebellion, and she would beg off, usually because she had the latest interesting job, and the rebellious Americans would move on, for reasons she never entirely understood. (Except she knew that they hadn't been fired.)

She put up with the passive-aggressive bigotry, and the frosty tones, and the arch comments about everything from her gender to her accent to her clothing, because she loved the work, although she had to admit that she had come to dread finishing the latest task, because that would mean another meeting with Ranklesworth and his team.

This meeting was no different. She knew that she wouldn't be praised for proving yet another impossible task to be possible, but she would like Ranklesworth and his team to at least put a chair at the table for her, so she wouldn't stand like an angular, overly tall, badly cast supplicant out of a high school production of *Oliver!*

Because that was another of the problems. In addition to being the only female mage in the building, she was also the tallest, thinnest person here. Six-two when she was barefoot, taller when she wore her favorite pair of leather-tooled cowboy boots, she was also the only person who still had actual color in her hair.

And that color happened to be a rich, dark amber—not flaming red, really, but not brown either. One of those colors that women usually bought out of a bottle. Dallas never messed with it, not even as strange hair colors like hot pink and green came into vogue. She usually wore her hair pulled away from her face, although today, she let it down, because something about these meetings made her want to seem more female rather than less.

Her eyes were that same amber and her skin wasn't much lighter. If someone had done a genetic test of her past, they would have found every single category of Texan in her DNA—from Comanche to Spanish to Mexican to white. She hadn't lived in Texas in more than a hundred and fifty years, but she carried it with her, in her dress (she favored bolo ties when forced to wear a tie), her accent, and her DNA.

She clearly did not fit in, and she wasn't quite sure why the men hadn't told her that from the beginning. She liked to think it was because they were stunned by her presence—an uppity woman of uncertain background who could outperform them on every single task. They kept trying to best her, and they never could.

One of the Americans hired a few decades ago told her they kept her because she ticked every diversity box. And she had raised her eyebrows at him: *When you can solve problems as easily as I can*, she had said, *I will accept your theory.*

He had been gone long before that theory could ever be tested.

Still, as the world changed around her, she wondered why she stayed here. Maybe there was a bit of ego involved for her as well. She liked besting the bigots. She liked proving to them over and over and over again that she was the best at what they all did, and that they could never find a job that was impossible for her to do.

Although this new job had an odd feel, right from the beginning.

First, the men were laughing as she came through the door. The nine Ranklesworth clones had a rather gusty way of laughing, all nose and closed-mouth hilarity. The two Americans (as she still called them, even though she really should have used their names) actually giggled, which wasn't really a good look on them when they were trying to be as fusty as their colleagues.

They were holding green-and-red folders that looked out of place three days before the beginning of the Fourth of July holiday (Ranklesworth insisted on celebrating every holiday, even when the holiday celebrated his country's defeat). She had a feeling that the men thought that this time—*this time*—they had finally found the project that would defeat her.

Since they thought that every single time they brought her a project, and she always proved that she was more capable than they thought, they shouldn't have been so mirthful. And they usually weren't. They usually watched her with beady-eyed uncertainty, trying to figure out if they had found the right project to get her out of the company.

This time, though. This time, they seemed certain of it.

She clomped into the room, her boot heels slapping on the polished concrete floor. She had long ago stopped asking that another chair be brought into the room. Instead, she stood, towering over them as if she were the one running the meeting.

On this day, she had chosen to wear a rather flirty, sky-blue skirt, with ruffles along the hem, and a sedate ivory blouse over it. That blue skirt said *female* in ways she couldn't, and that ivory blouse showed off not just the assets that Ranklesworth had once commented on (inappropriately, but before the mortal laws changed to disallow that sort of thing), but the assets that she was actually proud of—her toned arms and her surprisingly narrow waist. (Surprising to her, because she loved to eat. So she would enjoy the narrow as long as she could maintain it—without magic.)

The laughing stopped when she stopped at the head of the table—or rather, the foot of the table, since Ranklesworth was directly across from her.

Half of the Ranklesworth clones looked at her as if they had never seen her before, and the other half looked at her as if they couldn't wait to see her brought down. The two Americans had stopped giggling, and weren't looking at her at all. They were examining those strange red-and-green file folders.

"Well, nice of you to join us, Miss Demaris," Ranklesworth said, with an emphasis on the *Miss*. He hated calling her by her last name, something she had insisted upon during their very first meeting, more than 100 years ago.

Mr. Ranklesworth, she had said primly, *I do hope you run this office in a professional manner. I expect to be addressed the way you'd address any other colleague, with an honorific, instead of using my given name. Unless this company uses everyone's given name...?*

He had flushed, but had called her Miss Demaris ever since. With an emphasis on the *Miss* to let the others know that she was female, yes, and also unmarried, which, apparently, he found to be as irregular as her female status.

His tone on this day implied that she was late, which she was not. The meeting was scheduled for the top of the hour, which was still five minutes away. For decades, he had played this passive-aggressive game with her of letting her know the incorrect time for a meeting. He had always done the same with the Americans, but on this day, apparently, they had gotten the right memo.

She had stopped worrying about it. Mr. Ranklesworth couldn't fire her, much to his chagrin, since the company had deemed her one of the most important employees it had ever had. She had had that designation since the dawn of the combustion engine, and it had only become more important in the years since she solved the computer and handheld device problems.

The company had called her to their London office just once, and there, a wizened little man who actually looked like a wizard should look had offered her the job of Director— Ranklesworth's job—but she had declined. She knew that she wasn't good at bossing people about. She was much better at making sure machines and magic worked well together, and she had said so.

The wizened little man—whose name she was not allowed

to know—had nodded, and had tried to grin, even though his grin got lost in the folds of his face.

Ranklesworth is jealous of you, and will do anything to get rid of you, the wizened little man said. *Rest assured that will never happen. But you will be subject to his whims if you don't replace him in the job.*

She thought she could handle the whims. After all, she had been handling them for more than a century now.

But occasionally, they grew tiring. Like today.

"This is our new job," Ranklesworth said, waving the red-and-green folder. "The command comes from on high. I tried to turn the work down, but wasn't allowed to. We are stuck with this project—or rather, you are, since you're our go-to gal."

She didn't wince when he said that. He'd adopted it over the last fifty years, and it still grated. It sounded like he was making fun of her accent and her gender whenever he said it. (And her competence. Always her competence.)

"May I have a folder?" she asked as she swiped a folder out of the hands of the nearest Ranklesworth clone. They were conveniently one folder short, which was a stupid trick they had played more often than she cared to think about.

The folder was thick with materials. All of the jobs arrived in the office on paper. She had arranged a way to get email and had a computer that could print out anything the group needed, but no one ever asked. The entire company preferred to use old-fashioned delivery services to deliver jobs in black embossed British letter-sized boxes embossed with gold foil.

She found those pretty a century ago, quaint sixty years ago, and tiresomely stuck in the past now.

An embossed candy cane was printed in the lower right hand corner of the front of the folder. There were no other words on the front at all.

She opened the interior, and some red, white, silver, and

green sparkles plumed out, accompanied by a cheerful little tinkle of music, as if she were in a cartoon and she had just received a magical gift.

She sighed, and hoped she wouldn't be tainted by any unwanted magic. She would have to check later.

The first page floated upward and created a lovely snow-filled scene, slightly larger than the folder itself. The scene included one of those fluffy snowfalls that everyone (except her) agreed was the perfect snowfall—big fat flakes that floated lazily down and landed on snowdrifts as if directed there by some algorithm.

Shoved deep in the snowdrifts were gigantic candy canes that served as some kind of gate, and beyond it, barely visible through the lovely snowfall, were the words *Claus & Company*.

She closed the folder on the image. It vanished, leaving the crisp scent of new-fallen snow behind.

"What is this?" she asked, even though she had a hunch she knew. They had brought her jobs like this before, in which she had lost half a productive day watching some advertising gimmick, instead of learning what the job was. Those gimmicks always put her behind.

"You," Ranklesworth said in a tone even more plummy than usual, "are going to the North Pole."

She let out half a laugh and set the folder on the table. "Yeah, sure. Let's cut through the hazing, and get to the actual job, shall we?"

The two Ranklesworth clones sitting closest to him started to snicker. That wasn't a good sign.

"That is the actual job," Ranklesworth said, his lips puckered ever so slightly, as if he was trying to hold back an uncharacteristic smile. "You are going to the North Pole to fix their computer system."

"The North Pole," she said. "The geographic North Pole?

The one with the constantly shifting ice that makes it impossible to live there?"

Ranklesworth let out a noise that sounded suspiciously like a raspberry. He was too dignified to release an actual raspberry, wasn't he? And wasn't a raspberry an American sound of disgust, not a British one?

"For the sake of the magical universe," he said when he got his puckered lips under control, "I would never send anyone to the—what did you call it? The 'geographic North Pole.' That's as uninteresting to me as the 'real' Mount Olympus. No, Miss Demaris. I am sending you to the *actual* North Pole. Santa's North Pole. I want you to fix his computer system."

"Santa isn't real," she said, and everyone in the entire room swung their heads toward her as if she had just said that magic wasn't real.

"I assure you," Ranklesworth said, "Santa is real."

"Well," Dallas said, "if he is real, I have issues with working for him. He allows children to go to sleep in need every night. He doesn't give out gifts to a goodly portion of the world. And he seems to favor the wealthy over everyone else."

"I don't really care what your political beliefs are, Miss Demaris," Ranklesworth said. "The fact is that his computer system is malfunctioning and he needs a magical/machine tech. I must tell you that all of the Christmas holiday is on our shoulders here. If we fail—well, if *you* fail—no child will get a visit from Santa Claus this year."

The laughter had left the room. The men were all staring at her nervously. And if Ranklesworth was telling the truth, then this might actually be a job that could get her fired if she failed.

"No," Dallas said.

"No?" Ranklesworth asked.

She nodded. "No," she repeated.

"No what?" he asked.

"No, I will not take this job. I despise snow and cold. I

refuse to go anywhere that has candy canes for gates, and I want nothing to do with this Claus & Company."

Ranklesworth let out a gusty sigh. His bushy eyebrows rose into his messy hair and, for once, his mustache actually looked like it was the right length.

"Well," he said, "I'm afraid you don't get to say no."

"Why not?" she asked. "I have never turned down a job before. In more than a century, I've done exactly what you've asked."

Even when it was stupid. Even when it was designed to make me fail. She thought that part, but didn't say any of it.

"Because this order didn't come from me." Ranklesworth's beady little eyes met hers. "It came from my boss."

"Tell him no," she said. "Or I will."

Ranklesworth closed his eyes for a moment, and she could almost read the thought balloon over his head: *Save me from uncooperative females.* Or something a bit harsher, something she didn't exactly want to see.

Ranklesworth took a deep breath, opened his eyes, and then said, "He asked for you by name. He said you are the very best person for the job."

"This job?" she asked, surprised. Ranklesworth had given her a reluctant compliment.

"Any job, really," Ranklesworth said tiredly. He clearly did not want to admit that. "You do have a higher success rate than anyone in the company."

She inclined her head toward him. Ranklesworth had never acknowledged that before.

The Ranklesworth clones were looking at him in shock. The Americans were looking at her in shock.

She wasn't sure exactly how to respond, so she didn't say anything.

"But yes, this job," Ranklesworth said. "He would say it was impossible, but he knows you've done the impossible before."

"Oh, for god's sake," she said. She *had* done the impossible. She took pride in the impossible. But she didn't want to do this. She didn't want this job at all.

It was the very first job they had ever told her to take that she was declining. And she was going to decline it forcefully, by giving Ranklesworth what he always wanted.

She took a deep breath, and said, "I'll quit before I go up there."

The clones' heads swiveled toward her. A few of the clones grinned at her, as if they had finally won a big prize. The Americans looked panicked.

Ranklesworth rolled his eyes. His lips thinned and then he shook his head, as if he couldn't believe what he had just heard.

"Much as I would love to accept your resignation," Ranklesworth said, "it's not possible here."

The clones' heads swiveled again, now looking at him in shock. The Americans frowned at him.

She did too. Ranklesworth should have jumped at the chance to get rid of her.

She braced the fingers of one hand against the cool wood of the conference table, feeling a bit breathless. They wouldn't let her quit? She had always kept that in her back pocket, just in case they stopped giving her interesting work.

That was the thing Ranklesworth never understood: he wasn't ever going to get rid of Dallas if he continued to give her impossible tasks. He would have gotten rid of her decades ago if he relegated her to a desk and treated her like the clones.

Although, this particular impossible job was getting rid of her, wasn't it? Even though, Ranklesworth said that wasn't possible.

"You've wanted to get rid of me for decades," she said.

Ranklesworth raised those bushy eyebrows, as if her comment had surprised him. It probably had. Not because he wanted to get rid of her, but because she knew about it.

"Accept my resignation, and send one of these gentlemen to the North Pole," she said.

One of the Americans actually turned his chair slightly, as if he was trying to get Ranklesworth's attention, but knew better than to interrupt.

"Can't," Ranklesworth said. "This is some kind of magical emergency, an all-hands-on-deck sort of thing. You'd be drafted even if you quit. It is, I'm told, the case of having the right person in the right job."

He sounded sincere, but she had no idea if he really was. She might have believed him if he had supported her work in the past. But he hadn't, and if she went by personal experience alone, she had to assume this was some kind of game, cleverly designed to make her the loser.

"I think I'll go to London and talk to your boss," she said. That man was the wizened little man she had met once before. He had seemed to like her, even if there were so many rules around his august personage that she half-felt like she had visited some kind of royalty.

Negotiating rules like that made her nervous, but she would do it in this instance.

"Do so," Ranklesworth said. "But bring warm clothing. They might just send you north straightaway from the London offices."

She frowned. That sounded true too. She'd actually seen it happen before. The previous Americans had gone to complain about something and never returned. They had been sent elsewhere, straight away from the London offices.

That could happen to her, even if London didn't send her to the North Pole. She might never return to Malibu, to her beach and her sky and her ocean.

That might just break her heart.

The others were quiet. The Americans were looking down, as if they were embarrassed or worried.

"Why aren't any of you fighting for this job?" she asked. She'd seen that before on the really important ones.

"Santa has a reputation," Ranklesworth said. "It's not a good one."

"Yeah, I noticed," she said.

"Not for the reasons you mentioned," Ranklesworth said. "But because he's...um...notoriously difficult for mages to work with."

"He doesn't like us much," one of the Americans said to the tabletop.

"Then why are we helping him?" Dallas asked.

"Because the magical underpinning of the universe is at stake," Ranklesworth said, as if she were the dumbest person on Earth.

That tone, she recognized. She had heard it in almost every conversation she'd had with Ranklesworth, particularly when it dealt with the way that mages and the so-called real world interacted.

She didn't ask, *What did I miss?* because that question put her in a one-down position. But she didn't exactly know how to ask what she needed to ask, so she settled on a good old American standby.

"Huh?" she asked.

Heads swiveled, except for the Americans. One continued to look down. The other put the back of his fingers against his forehead, shielding his face from everything going on at the table, the way that kids sometimes did when they were trying to become invisible.

"You really don't know this?" Ranklesworth asked. Then he shook his head, and repeated more to himself than to her, "You really don't know this."

He sighed gustily, shook his head again, and said, "Belief in magic powers magic."

Her eyes narrowed. She knew that. Of course she knew

that. That was why some of the older so-called gods had less power than some of the other so-called gods. Why certain cultures thrived in certain environments, like the Faerie Kings in Las Vegas. There, the irrational belief in luck powered most of their magical devices.

Dallas had used that luck-belief once, on a job that had taken her in the bowels beneath the city, to an astonishing and crazy Faerie King casino that had literally made her head spin.

But she knew better than to remind Ranklesworth that she couldn't do her job if she didn't understand what added fuel to magic's fire.

"Millions and millions of children believe in Santa Claus," Ranklesworth told her. "For each child that ages out of the belief, another is born into the belief. The mortal culture perpetuates that belief and is complicit in making sure that children under the age of five or so all believe it."

"They don't all believe it," she said unable to keep silent. "The 'culture,' as you call it, is at best what you used to call Western culture, at worst a purely American branding episode that focuses on children raised in a Christian—"

"Really," Ranklesworth said, "I told you, no politics."

"It's not politics," she said. "It's fact—"

"I don't care," Ranklesworth said. "It's a job that we have to do."

"Then find someone else. Because I refuse." She slammed the folder on the table and walked out of the conference room, not even stopping to look at her lovely ocean.

Ranklesworth could deal with his bosses.

Because she was done.

I value honest feedback, and would love to hear your opinion in a review, if you're so inclined, on your favorite book retailer's site.

Be the first to know!

Just sign up for the Kristine Kathryn Rusch newsletter, and keep up with the latest news, releases and so much more—even the occasional giveaway.

So, what are you waiting for? To sign up go to kristinekathrynrusch.com.

But wait! There's more. Sign up for the WMG Publishing newsletter, too, and get the latest news and releases from all of the WMG authors and lines, including Kristine Grayson, Kris Nelscott, Dean Wesley Smith, *Fiction River: An Original Anthology Magazine, Smith's Monthly,* and so much more.

To sign up go to wmgpublishing.com.

ABOUT THE AUTHOR

Called "The Reigning Queen of Paranormal Romance" by *Best Reviews,* bestselling author Kristine Grayson has made a name for herself publishing light, slightly off-skew romance novels about Greek Gods, fairy tale characters, and the modern world.

She writes historical mysteries as Kris Nelscott, and she also writes in a variety of genre, from literary to science fiction to romance, under her real name—Kristine Kathryn Rusch. She has won dozens of awards for her writing

As Kristine Grayson, she also edits the romance volumes of *Fiction River: An Original Anthology Magazine.*

For more information about her work, go to the Kristine Grayson www.kristinegrayson.com and sign up for her newsletter.

www.ingramcontent.com/pod-product-compliance
Lightning Source LLC
Chambersburg PA
CBHW022031170626
46808CB00003B/1146